SECRETS OF KUNG FULIO

Written by:

TRENT KANIUGA
&
CHRIS KRUBECK

Artwork by:

TRENT KANIUGA & DANNY KONG

Additional Art: Domen Kozelj

Special Thanks:
ELIZABETH MOON
NICK COLE
JASON ANSPACH

1st Edition

SPERIA
EASTERN CONTINENT
WORLD MAP

MYSTIC LANDS

To the rest of Speria, the Eastern Continent is known as the "Mystic Lands", due to the stories of supernatural demons and ancient sorcery, sealed demon gates, and many other relics from a forgotten age. Because of that, many bandits and theives travel to these lands in hopes of disappearing forever.

Whereas most of the rest of the world has embraced technology, the Eastern continent rejected much of the automation and mechanization of the new world, and embraced a more spiritual pursuit. The lush mountains, and open fields preserve the old way of life for many farmers, small time merchants and fisherman. Small cities such as Belgarde exist as a central hub, but it pales in comparison to the meccas found in other continents.

Jubee's Rock House

Crescent Isle

TWILIGHT MONK

SECRETS OF KUNG FULIO

CHAPTER 1

THE NEW KID

Raziel Tenza ripped through the muddy back alleys of Crescent Isle. The taste of blood still in his mouth, he wondered what he'd ever done to deserve this.

This is the LAST time I stick my neck out for someone else! he thought to himself as he quickly gestured to his companion to slide under the low bridge behind him.

Even with a Moonken's heightened senses, Raz could barely hear their relentless pursuers over the deluge of rainfall and his own heavy breathing. His feet glided treacherously out from under him as he slid around the back of Hamcha's Barbeque, knocking over an unsuspecting cook on his late evening smoke break.

"Watch it, Moonken!" the rotund old man shouted angrily, waving his fist in the air. There wasn't time to stop and apologize. Even if he'd made the effort, it wouldn't

change anything. The people
in Crescent Isle
already had no love for Raziel,
and not much he'd done since
he
arrived seemed to change
their mind about that. Plus, he
had more significant problems
to consider.

Several paces behind
him, and struggling to keep
up, Rin Torra staggered
clumsily, panting with
exhaustion and shouting
unintelligibly. At first glance,
one would be forgiven for
mistaking the big Moonken
for a chef-in-training rather than a monk under the
tutelage of some of the most fearsome warriors in all of
Speria. In short, he was not the spitting image of martial
arts prowess. On most days, Rin carried his large frame
with surprising agility, but he had a knack for screwing up
at just the right moments. If bad timing were a talent, Rin
would be exceptional.

Seeing an opportunity to put some distance between
them and their pursuers, Raz kicked over a trash can and
hung a hard right into another narrow corridor, deeper
into the alleys and away from the central marketplace.
Moments later, a crash and a frustrated yell echoed against
the walls behind him. One of them yelled, "Dudes! I think
they went this way!"

"These guys don't quit!" Raz huffed as he pulled at
his companion's arm, darting over a railing and sliding
down into the lower street level.

The Celestial Temple loomed over them with mocking
indifference as they clumsily sped through the rain-soaked,
narrow back alleys. Raz's muscles threatened to give out
on him at any moment. He couldn't help but wonder what
good the six months of training at the monastery had done
for him. It hadn't awakened any kind of hidden Moonken

Raziel Tenza

Rin Torra

abilities, as he'd hoped, that was for sure. In fact, after all that he'd been through to get there, he'd decided that Crescent Isle was none of the things that he always hoped and dreamed of.

Unfamiliar with the more obscure back alleys, he'd inadvertently led them smack-dab into a fork in the road. Rin shouted something inaudibly in a panicked tone from behind him. Without thinking, Raz hung a right.

There was a sickening crunch, a flash of pain, and suddenly his feet were flying out from under him. Suspended in mid-air, he watched the shining raindrops and the blood from his nose splash together like jewels against the starry sky, reflecting off the giant pointed rock from which Crescent Isle drew its name.

For a brief moment, his view of the enormous crescent stone was quite beautiful, until he abruptly hit the muddy ground with a thud.

Sinister laughter erupted from a point somewhere in front of him. Raz stumbled clumsily to his feet and tried to shake the stars from his eyes.

At the end of the alley stood the blurry shadows of

three figures. Even in silhouette, the iconic curl of Nox's absurd, yet prized, long pompadour was unmistakable.

"The Red Cobras," Raz grumbled to himself. "What a stupid name."

Raz straightened himself up as best he could, wiped the blood from his nose, and resisted the urge to double over in exhaustion. Just behind him, Rin stumbled back a few steps further into the alley as if hoping to hide in Raz's shadow.

At first glance, you'd never know Nox was the leader of Crescent Isle's most ruthless underaged gang of thugs. He wasn't much taller than Raz, hair notwithstanding. What he lacked for in height, he made up for in strength and severity. His squat frame was bound tightly by well-trained muscle, and his square jaw permanently set his mouth into a self-satisfied grin.

He sauntered into the alley, flexing his exposed shoulders from under the torn red and black sleeves of his robes. Every muscle in Raz's body tensed. Rin nervously stumbled and fell onto his butt with a splash. He raised his hands over his face as if the blows were already raining down on him. A snicker escaped from Nox's two cronies.

Suck it up.

Raz prepared for what was coming with a quick reaffirming pep talk.

Push your chest out. Never let 'em see you get rattled. Never for a moment let 'em know that they've got the upper hand.

He planted both of his feet into the slick mud firmly. He didn't stand a chance, but he hoped that they didn't know that.

When everything is stacked against you, and whatever you're doing isn't working, that's when you have to double down.

Raz took a deep breath.

"I think he's had enough, jerk face," he growled at three other boys, in the most grumbly, tough-guy tone a fifteen-year-old newbie-monk-with-little-to-no-training-or-fighting-ability-whatsoever could muster.

"Ooooooooohhh!" the Cobras groaned in unison. Instead of laughing, one of them just giggled in a strangely high pitched voice that almost seemed like a squeal.

Nox chuckled then got in Raz's face. He was so close that Raz could smell Tomo's famous Tater stew on his breath. He began eyeballing him up and down. Sniffing. Not a normal sniff, but the weirdo kind. Like he was smelling for something in particular. He tilted his neck from side to side, and flicked his tongue, making snake-like slithering sounds.

"Thwwwwww thwwwww thwwww!"

Despite how uncomfortable he was, Raz did not flinch. It was a test, and he knew it.

"Outta the way, new kid," Nox whispered forcefully. "This kind of business don't concern you."

Raz stood firm. Nox tilted his head curiously. "Come on kid, why even get involved? You could still just... walk away. Yeah?"

Raz glanced back over his shoulder at Rin, who only covered his face, still shivering. "Jeez Rin, get up already. You're embarrassing me," he mumbled.

Seeing how scared Rin was, and knowing what was coming, Raz began to wonder why he'd bothered to stick up for the big guy to begin with. Nox was right; he could've just looked the other way. He'd merely picked the wrong alley to pass through on his way to dodging Master Klu's class again. But it all just didn't sit right with him. He couldn't sit back and watch these jerks kick the snot out of another kid who didn't deserve it, no matter how pathetic he might be.

"Not a chance," Raz snarled stubbornly. "A couple of pansies like you guys couldn't be that tough. Not if you need to bring your two boyfriends here to team up on one kid."

Rin shifted in the mud, growing more uncomfortable with every second, and covered his head.

Nox snarled, and without hesitation, drove his knee into Raz's groin. A spasm of pain erupted from his balls to the back of his neck. Then, once Raz was on the ground, Nox put a single finger to his nostril and blew, sending a yellowy string of mucus directly onto Raz's eyelid.

So much for looking tough.

By the time Raz regained his senses, the other Red Cobras had taken up their positions in the alley to surround the two of them. Diego was first, beady eyes flicking back and forth from Raz to Rin like a hungry fox wondering which defenseless chicken to eat first. His hair, dyed red from the usual Moonken white, was styled into a spiky mohawk, each point filled with enough hair gel to be a deadly weapon.

The third and largest member of Nox's terror squad was Bolo - bigger than Nox and Diego combined. If one were to cover Bolo's large frame in a layer of fur, he'd probably be mistaken for a wild ape. For reasons no one knew for sure, a small log was permanently embedded in the brute's bangs. No one dared ask him why. He stood like a fourth wall to the alley - a wall that could punch you so hard you'd forget your own name.

"I didn't know you two were so tight!" Nox proclaimed to his two victims.

"Awww, look at 'em, Nox! Fatty got himsewf a fwiend," Diego cooed sardonically. Raz winced, both from the pain and because he hated when bullies did the baby talk.

"More like tubby here squeezed one out," Nox sneered, scrunching his nose at them like they were another piece of discarded trash.

"Heh, heh. Smells like it," Bolo laughed in agreement. It wasn't the first time Raz had heard this joke. He highly doubted it would be the last. The Red Cobras had about half of a brain between all three of them, and most of their jokes consisted of boogers, farts and crap. Yeah, everything about them was gross.

Shakily, Raz rose to his feet once more and wiped the ooze off his face.

Diego

"Don't... you'll only make it worse," Rin whispered, gesturing for Raz not to get up. Raz didn't listen. He gritted his teeth and shook his head. Outmatched or not, Raz Tenza didn't lay down and give up for anyone.

"You shoulda stayed down, farm boy!" Nox threatened.

"You don't scare me, Nox," Raz growled in return, gritting his teeth defiantly.

"Ooooh, tough guy. Hear that, boys? He ain't scared!" Nox said, turning to his grinning stooges. He faced Raz again. "I saw you workin' on your moves behind Klu's dojo the other day. Very impressive," Nox teased.

"I think you ACTUALLY managed to HIT the target a few times!"

They all laughed. Raz flushed and averted his gaze. "Just because you had a ten-year head start on your training doesn't make you better than me," he grumbled bitterly.

"Hah! You could be trainin' for a HUNDRED years, and I could still beat you with my hands tied, newbie. You got NO talent."

Raz grumbled. "You don't know anything about me."

"Oh, I know you. I know EXACTLY what you are, country boy. From the second you showed up at the monastery, I had you pegged," Nox taunted, shoving his finger into Raz's chest. "I bet you think you're pretty special, don't you? I heard the rumors about you. 'The Beast of Tuksa'. Now, why in the heck would anyone call you that?" He opened his eyes wide in mock admiration. "Newsflash, butt wipe! There's NOTHING special about you! No one even WANTS you here! In fact, if you disappeared tomorrow, no one would even notice."

A pang spread through Raz's chest. There was some truth there. He'd come to the monastery far later than any of the other students. He'd taken a new name, and washed away the remnants of his old life, just like the others. But he could never wash away what he knew that he truly was. The Masters still seemed to treat him like he was only an inconvenience, the townspeople were indifferent, and the other students mostly ignored him. Everyone thought he was a joke.

"For someone who's just another student, you sure got a high opinion of yourself," Raz shot back, dragging himself out of his inner turmoil.

Nox swiveled sideways and rocketed his right foot into Raz's face, introducing the new student's backside to the mud once more. The Red Cobras roared with approving laughter.

"WRONG! This is MY island," Nox proclaimed. "And if you want a future here, you gotta go through ME."

Raz grimaced, spat out a mouthful of blood, and

attempted to wipe the footprint from his face. Nox
slammed his fists across his chest then spread them out
wide to either side.

"Red Cobras fricking RULE!" he roared. Diego
and Bolo repeated the same idiotic salute with deathly
seriousness.

Several stories above them, a window cracked open.
An older man in a fishing hat leaned on the windowsill,
puffing on a wooden pipe. Old Man Flannagan. He looked
down at the wet, bloody Moonken on the wall below him
with disinterest then slammed the window shut once more.

Typical.

Raz tried to raise himself off the ground, but Nox's
foot slammed his head back down and held it there,
suffocating him in cold, grimy alley water. The leader
of the Red Cobras blew out a big breath and seemingly
relaxed, propping his forearms casually on the knee that
held Raz's face under the puddle of water.

"You two ever read The Phantom Kids?" he
questioned out of the blue.

"N-No…" Rin stuttered and stiffly shook his head,
trying not to agitate him any further but knowing very
well he already had. "Nox, listen, we're sor—"

"Yo. How about you, new kid?" Nox asked, ignoring
Rin. He looked down at Raz, who gurgled and thrashed
under his foot. "Speak up, new kid! I can't hear you!"

He eased up on Raz's head just enough to let him
breathe. Raz coughed and gasped for air, figuring he
wouldn't have it for long.

"Man, The Phantom Kids was a great comic! Master
Klu used to bring us every issue," Nox went on casually.
"See, the Phantom Kids used their incredible ancient
powers to fight off all the evil, gross-looking monsters that
invaded their city. It had great art too man! Especially the
fight scenes."

"Yeah, that's super," Raz coughed, still fighting for air.
"Get to the point."

"Patience, newbie, patience," Nox continued.
Annoyed at the interruption, he put a bit more weight
on Raz's skull. "Ya see… every issue some new monster

would show up, and the Phantom kids? They would kill
the monster and save the day. Every. Single. Time. They
didn't win because of friendship or believing in themselves,
or some lame-ass crap like that. That's what made it such
a believable comic! See, they beat them because they were
the strongest. They were WINNERS! Get it? That's what
made 'em heroes! Just like my boys and me. We ALWAYS
win!"

"Now I wonder," Nox bent down so he was right next
to Raz's ear, "what's that make you?"

With a final humiliating shove, Nox released Raz's
head from the water and moved away. Raz rose to his
knees and wiped away yet another layer of bloody mud
and grime from his face. But with the back of his hand, he
only managed to smear it in more.

"I'm not sure what's worse," Raz hissed with a smirk.
"Getting hit in the balls or listening to you prattle on about
your stupid little comic."

Nox gave Raz a pitying shake of the head. He pulled
out a wad of well-chewed gum from his mouth and
squeezed it experimentally between two fingers.

"I knew you wouldn't get it. See, the monastery
used to be strong. WE... used to be strong." He raised
his elbow and squinted to line up the gum-wad with its
intended target, then slowly smashed the sticky, dripping
lump of gooey gum into the center of Raz's forehead and
held it there until it stuck firmly. "But we just keep getting
stuck," he continued in a low, exhausted groan, "with
weak ass pansies like you two. That's the whole reason
why I had to start the Red Cobras, to separate the winners
from the losers. As the strongest student at the monastery,
it's practically my job to take out the garbage... like you
two."

"Your job? Peh! You wouldn't talk so big if the
Masters were here," Raz fired back.

"Pffft! Do you think I'm scared of the Masters?
Those old geezers are pacifists! Besides," Nox glanced
over his shoulder casually, "I don't see any Masters here
anyway, do you?"

Raz was at a loss for any kind of response. The Red

Cobras could probably tear the market to pieces, and the Masters wouldn't even bat an eye.

"I got BIG plans in the works for Crescent Isle, BIG PLANS. Stuff that's gonna be legendary," Nox proclaimed, flexing his muscles. "When we're done, it's gonna be the Masters who are scared of us."

Raz cocked an eyebrow as the Cobras roared with laughter once more. Apparently, they really believed it.

Before he'd arrived at Crescent Isle, everyone talked about it like it was this great place where Moonken all lived in harmony and sang happy songs around a campfire every night. But no matter where he went in Speria, it seemed that someone was always there to look down their nose at him, to make sure people stayed in their lane. Invariably, people with power crushed those weaker than them just because they could.

"You talk a big game, but someday, someone's gonna take you down and show the world what you REALLY are," Raz said before his brain had time to stop him. The Red Cobras stopped laughing. Even Rin stopped cowering for a second to look up at him from the ground, eyes full of wonder.

Then, the smile returned to Nox's face. He cackled loudly, as though Raz had just told the funniest joke in the world.

"Hahaha! Look at the balls on the new kid; I love it!" he laughed for an instant before the smile disappeared once more. "But I know the truth about you."

Raz stumbled for a moment. "Yeah? And what's that?"

Nox grinned back at him. "All bark and no bite." He turned his back to

Raz, towards the center of the alley and moved to stand over Rin instead. Bolo and Diego moved in obediently behind him. Rin tried to squirm away but didn't get far before Nox dug his foot into his back and held him in place.

"I swear, you're pathetic Rin. Did you really think this worthless loser was going to protect you? What were you thinking? He's a damn nobody. Even if he wanted to, he couldn't do anything. He's even more pathetic than you," Nox finally sighed.

Raz glanced at the opening in the alley where Bolo had been. He could have escaped. They'd given him his chance to run. But in that moment, he wasn't thinking about Rin, or his training, or how his guts hurt. He wasn't even thinking about the blood running down his face.

He's a nobody...

Those words echoed in his mind. His fists curled into tight balls; his jaw clamped down as every instinct in his being urged him to hit Nox between his stupid, beady eyes.

The combined feelings from years of being kicked down formed a pit of rage inside of him. He felt the anger rise for all of the people that had let him down, and for this stupid island that promised everything and gave him nothing, and for every falling star that didn't land in the ass-end of nowhere. But more than anything, he felt the hatred of every self-righteous bully that had ever thrown a rock at him or poked him with a stick.

He couldn't do anything...

So many times he'd heard those words before, but this time, coming from Nox, it really hit home.

Raz's body began tensing up so much that he started to shake. His teeth rattled. His arms began to twitch. Not because he was afraid, he'd never been afraid of anything. No. It was because he knew Nox was right about him. He felt that all those things he said were true.

But not tonight. Tonight, he'd had enough.

Before he could even think, his arm spun out from his side. Every ounce of rage he had was riding on that fist. It contained all of the vengeance for every injustice, against every bully that ever spat on him, spiraling at full speed right towards Nox's nose. It wasn't just a punch. It was old-school justice. Pure, old school justice for every downtrodden bum that ever got kicked around.

The fist flung through the air at tremendous speed but never hit its target. Nox caught it in mid-air and held it there. It was almost as if he knew what was going to happen before it did.

Crap.

Without a word, Nox studied Raz's fist with both surprise and amusement. Then, he burst into laughter, followed by the rest of his goons.

"So PATHETIC! Hah hah! You can't even throw a decent punch!"

Holding Raz's fist in his hand, he started twisting. A sting of pain shot all the way up Raz's arm and down his neck. The pain was unbearable. His arm felt like it was going to snap. To ease the strain, his body buckled automatically to the ground, smacking his face into the mud.

By now, a few more humans, Barrakewdos, Parpaks and every other kind of creature that had migrated from all over Speria to Crescent Isle had poked their heads out of the surrounding windows or around the corner above the alley to get a front-row seat to the Moonken brawl.

Nox fumed and looked around at the new spectators, his breath puffing out of his nose like an enraged bull. He made eye contact with Bolo and Diego and shook his head. They dropped Rin into the muddy water with a thud right beside Raz. They laid so firmly together, their noses almost touched.

"Alright, enough messin' around," Nox announced. Flexing, he inspecting his own muscles proudly as he stood over the two of them. "I'm the garbage man, and you're the garbage." Clapping his hands together, he squatted down until he was hovering just above his helpless victims. "Listen up, losers!" He knelt down and slapped Rin across the cheek. "I already told you ONCE to get off my island tubby. But you don't seem to hear so good. And seeing you tonight only proves to me, that you're even more useless than I thought."

Rin's words unintelligibly caught in his throat. Overwhelmed with fear, all he managed to do was to shake his head in the mud.

"Oh, stop squirmin', lil' piggy. Truth be told, I was kinda worried about you out there all by your lonesome in the big open world, but now it looks like you're gonna have your new pal to keep you company out there," he said then glanced over at Raz. "I gotta admit... I actually kinda like your spirit new kid! Stupid, but gutsy. It takes an awful lot to impress me, so I'm gonna cut you both a little slack."

"Which... means...?" Raz gasped between painful breaths.

"I'm glad you asked," Nox said with a grin. He shoved a finger into the air. "One more day. I'll give you both until sundown tomorrow to get off Crescent Isle and out of my sight, for good."

"Leave Crescent Isle...?" Rin asked in a stupor. "And go where? This is our home!"

Nox chuckled with amusement. "I don't give a damn where you go. Go cuddle up to a tree or camp in the woods for all I care, as long as you're off my island."

"What if we don't go?" Raz knew that asking questions now wasn't going to help his situation and that even

opening his mouth was asking for more pain, but the way he saw it, he couldn't be in more pain than he already was.

A sickening smile spread across Nox's lips.

"Well, then today's little session will be a nice memory compared to what we do to you next time."

"Gee. Thanks," Raz mumbled into the mud.

In one fluid motion, Nox grabbed Raz and tossed him across the alley and into an open trash can. His limbs contorted painfully as he was wedged inside the narrow space.

"Perfect shot, boss," Bolo grunted with approval. The world went dark as the large Moonken slammed the lid shut on top of Raz. His body cried out in aching protest as Diego gave the can one last savage kick.

"Consider today a warning, new kid. But the next time you feel like being a tough guy, remember this: little crybaby wannabees who get in my way don't have a future on Crescent Isle. Especially if they're as weak and frail as you two. Let's go, Cobras. These losers have got some packing to do," Nox concluded by snapping his fingers. The Red Cobras pushed through the crowd that had formed as they marched out of the alley.

Moments later, light-flooded Raz's eyes as the trash can lid finally lifted once more.

"Raz! You alright?" Rin's fuzzy face doubled and swirled in circles above him.

"Yeah, feelin' fine... hey, quit spinnin' around s' much," Raz slurred, barely holding on to consciousness. As the sounds of the world got tinny and distant and his head swam with stars, Raz could hear the laughter of the Red Cobras fading away into the distance.

Then, everything went black.

CHAPTER 2

THE BIG GUY

"HEY! Wake up!" Raz felt a light slap from the back of a hand against his wet cheek. When he opened his eyes, Rin's big dopey blur of a face smiled over him.

As the world faded back in, so did the pain. A dull ache pulsated throughout Raz's entire body, from the tips of his toes to his forehead, punctuated by sharp intense twinges from an old shoulder wound from years past whenever he moved.

"Thank god! I thought you were dead!" Rin exclaimed then fell back, heaving a big sigh of relief.

"Dead...? How long was I out?!"

"Long enough to have me worried," Rin explained. "What I meant is that you looked dead. That's to say, you look terrible. Like really gross. Like —"

"Thanks. I get the picture," Raz interjected. "At least YOU got off without a scratch,"

"Thanks to you," Rin stated, oblivious to Raz's bitter jab. "Oh! Are you hungry? I bet you're hungry. One sec!" He scuttled off before Raz could reply. It sure was dark.

Grunting, Raz reached over to turn on the lamp at his bedside but slapped the floor instead. Odd. Why was his mattress on the floor? Raz sniffed the musty air.

He quickly realized that this wasn't his room in the monastery. Immediately to his right was a short table. He strained in the darkness to get a better look.

It was covered in homemade throwing knives, metal balls attached to ropes, some sort of grenade, knives attached to ropes - why were there so many ropes?

Abruptly, and very painfully, he shot up to a sitting position. A flash of lightning briefly illuminated the room.

"What the…?"

Every vertical surface of the room was covered in handwritten notes, diagrams, and posters of black-clad people wielding nefarious weapons. Hundreds of implements were scattered across the floor: black robes, stakes, adhesives, ball bearings, caltrops, wires, ropes - more ropes! Suppressing the urge to run for his life, Raz turned over and picked up some sort of pointy object. It almost looked like… a ninja star?

"Pretty cool, right...?" Rin muttered directly behind Raz's ear.

"GAH!" Raz yelled in surprise, unable to defend himself.

A light clicked on. In Raz's hand was indeed a ninja star, albeit one made of string, tape, and shark's teeth.

"I made it all myself!" Rin stated proudly then threw a sandwich onto Raz's chest. Far from an evil torture dungeon, Raz found himself surrounded by an incredible display of homemade ninja paraphernalia.

"Uhhh... yeah. Really cool," he muttered, hoping to placate the big guy in case he turned out to be unstable.

"What is all this stuff?" he asked.

Rin looked side to side conspiratorially as if someone might be listening through the floorboards.

"No one's supposed to know about all this, but…" He rummaged through the satchel that was forever at his waist, pulled out a magazine, and held it up to Raz's face. "Check out this bad boy!"

Raz studied the cover, a woman in a bikini, although her face was concealed by a black mask. "Ninja Arts Weekly... Swimsuit Edition," he read aloud slowly. "Aren't ninja arts forbidden by the Masters?"

Rin scrunched his face in disgust and snatched the magazine back to his chest defensively. Clearly, this was a sensitive topic.

"Well, that's why I said no one knows about it! Do I gotta spell it out for you?! Jeeez!" he complained, slapping the cover with the back of his hand. "You're the first person I've ever brought here, so you're the only one that knows!"

"I am?" It wasn't often anyone in the monastery trusted Raz with anything important, even his roommate.

"Yup! Well if you can't trust your closest buddy, then who can you trust?" Rin asked mysteriously. Raz arched an eyebrow - he wasn't sure if he was ready to be anyone's *closest buddy*.

"And where is 'here', exactly?" he asked, avoiding the subject.

"You know that big wooden owl on top of Yuelai's Clothing Store?"

"You mean that tacky wooden monstrosity?" Raz clarified.

"That's the one!"

"Yeah, I know it. What about it?"

Rin gestured to the walls. "We're in it."

In his initial shock Raz had completely glossed over the odd shape of the room. The weirdly angular and nonsensical layout started to make a strange sense. There wasn't just one circular window but two. One for each eye of the owl.

They were in the middle of the market courtyard - only minutes from the alley. Now reoriented, he could hear the sounds of the food stalls, trinket vendors, the bathhouse, and other shops still operating below them.

"Wait a minute, you're telling me you had this crazy hideout the whole time I was here?" Raz asked, dumbfounded and somewhat impressed that the big dope had managed to hide such a big secret from him all that time.

"Shadowmaster Kito says the number one rule of stealth is to hide in plain sight," Rin replied proudly, passing his fingers over the text of the magazine lovingly.

Raz forced his swollen right eye open and poked at his own head, finding it covered in strange lumps and scratches. It felt like Nox had literally beat his face off and replaced it an unfamiliar mask. Luckily, in the time it took to drag Raz

to the hideout many of the bruises had already turned in color from a deep purple to a sickly yellow. If it wasn't for the healing abilities of a Moonken, he probably wouldn't be able to open his eyes at all.

Rin licked his lips and averted his eyes like he was embarrassed about something.

"Hey, about what you did for me back there. That was…"

Raz smiled and waved his hand dismissively. "Don't mention it, it was—"

"… Pretty stupid," Rin finished, instantly deflating Raz's ego. "Still, thanks for sticking your neck out for me. Not many people have the guts to talk back to Nox like you did. Those that do…well," he paused and studied the state of Raz's face, "they end up looking a lot like you. Or worse."

"Don't mention it," Raz mumbled.

"So, what's the plan, buddy? We need to figure out what to do next," Rin stated casually in the same tone someone would ask you about what you wanted for dinner.

"We?" Raz retorted.

"Well, you're going to need my help if you're planning to take down Nox," Rin said.

Raz's face scrunched in confusion, which hurt like hell.

"What the heck are you talking about? Who said anything about taking out Nox?!"

"You did, remember?" Rin reminded him. "Right before he dunked you in the trash can and right after you failed spectacularly to punch him in the face."

"Gee, thanks for reminding me," Raz said sarcastically, rising to his elbows. "Just because I said someone should take him down a peg doesn't mean that someone should be us."

"B-But nobody else has stood up to Nox like that! Not ever!"

"Yeah, and look where it got me," Raz said, pointing to

his swollen face.

"But…" Rin trailed off in utter confusion. "What are we gonna do?"

Raz frowned, wishing he could say what Rin clearly wanted him to. But facts were facts.

"You heard what Nox said: *leave Crescent Isle or else*, with a big emphasis on the *'or else'*."

"And?"

"Listen, I'm not interested in fighting your war with this guy. As soon as I can get out of this bed, I'm getting my stuff…" Raz took a deep, painful breath.

Rin waited with wide eyed anticipation.

"… and I'm GETTING OFF THIS STUPID ISLAND! I am LEAVING!" Raz shouted bitterly.

Rin scampered over and slid to a stop next to the mattress, his eyes wide with shock. "What? No way! You can't!"

"Watch me!" Raz declared and confidently rose to his feet only to come crashing back down to the mattress as a painful spasm traveled up his thigh into his back.

So much for a dramatic exit.

"You can't just LEAVE!" Rin whined.

"Why not?" Raz argued. "I've never belonged here anyways. The Masters already made up their mind about me, and so has everyone else. They think I'm a lost cause… and a loser."

"Well… I don't think you're a loser," Rin said defensively.

Meeting Rin's sad puppy dog eyes, Raz couldn't help but sigh. As far as he could tell the big guy actually believed it.

"Oh yeah? Tell that to all the students laughing behind my back, or the Masters when they talk down to me like I'm just some stupid kid," Raz scoffed.

Rin shook his head. "Naw buddy! That's just because

you're new! When everyone doubts you, all you gotta do is prove yourself and they'll change their minds," he jumped excitedly onto the mattress.

"Yeah? And how's that gonna happen?! Maybe you haven't noticed... but you and me? We're pretty awful at fighting."

Rin nodded solemnly in agreement, much to Raz's annoyance. He could have at least tried to deny it. "Well, your fighting skills are... not great. Pretty bad, honestly."

"I'm sorry, maybe my memory's a little fuzzy, but I didn't see you doing much to help me out back there," Raz said defensively.   Rin plucked up the copy of Ninja Arts Weekly off the floor, and turned to a section in the middle so quickly it must've been memorized. He shoved his finger at it and continued. "Shadowmaster Kito says that you should always do whatever you can to fight another day, even if that means making a tactical retreat."

"Is that what you call cowering behind me? A 'tactical retreat'?" Raz wondered.

"Ummm..." Rin went red, his eyes darted to the floor as he did his best to ignore the question. "But hey, you know you'll never become a great fighter if you leave now!"

The hairs on the back of Raz's neck stood on end. Being a Moonken, he knew that he didn't stand much of a chance outside of Crescent Isle. But a Moonken monk who could fight... that was a whole different story.

Raz shook the thought from his head.

"Doesn't matter. Guys like Nox... when they smell weakness, they prey on it and kick you down until there's nothing left. As long as he's around, there'll never be a place for us here. He'll make sure of that."

Rin's face sank and went pale. He sat in silence, looking down at the floor again in defeat just like he had in the alley earlier that night.

"This isn't the only island in the world, you know," Raz reasoned. "Why don't you come with me?"

Even in the low light, Raz could see Rin was shaking and his eyes began to tear up.

"I CAN'T!" Rin shouted, angrily wiping tears away from his eyes. "You wouldn't understand!"

"What's so important?" Raz said as gently as he could. "Why stay? For the training?"

"No. It's not that," Rin replied with such gravity that it made Raz pause. "Look around you. This island is the home of over four thousand years of Moonken history! I don't know what you saw out there before you came to Crescent Isle, Raz. But for me, before... I got to see a few of those other fancy places, too."

Quietly, he untied the tightly fitted black cloth that was always on his head. In six months, Raz had never seen Rin without it. Not at training, or while they ate, not even when he went to the bathhouse. Hesitantly, Rin parted a tuft of hair, revealing a long, unsightly scar stretching from his left ear to the center of his forehead.

"You know as well as I do," he said, meeting Raz's eye, "Moonken don't belong out there. THIS is where we belong. The world's full of people like Nox. At least here, we know where the rocks are gonna come flying from." He tucked his hair back under the cloth. Before Raz could speak, Rin was on his feet.

"So fine!" Rin stomped defiantly. "If you wanna run away, go ahead and leave! And if I can't go... I mean... if I'm on my own I'm..." His eyes darted back and forth while he outlined all of the possibilities in his mind. "I'll have to find a way to stand up to the Cobras and defend Crescent Isle on my OWN!" he said with tears in his eyes.

His hands began to shake, until he just collapsed to the ground and outright started sobbing. It was the kind of sobbing where every other word is a hard swallow. It was the kind of sobbing that would shake the foundation of anyone with a soul that ever gave a damn about another poor hard luck sap.

As Raz stood there with the big guy, rain pattering against the ceiling of the owl hideout, he starting to think stupid thoughts. If he left Crescent Isle for good, he'd be letting down all the Moonken. If there was some divine reason why he ended up here, he'd be walking away from that too. But more than any of that, he'd be dooming this poor kid to a lifetime of wedgies and bloody noses... or worse. There was no telling how far Nox would go.

It was an old, familiar pain he felt rising up inside him. There was no way Rin could survive on his own. He couldn't just walk away knowing that he could've done something to stop it. It was a regret that he would not be able to live with.

It was probably just a coincidence, but at that very moment, outside the window the rain subsided into a drizzle, and the dark clouds above slowly parted like curtains on a stage, revealing a full, ringed moon all aglow. Halo and everything.

"Damn. I never shoulda got involved," Raz mumbled as he looked through the circular windows.

Before Raz could really think it through, his mouth was already moving. "OK. Hypothetically..." he began.

Hearing the change in Raz's tone, Rin's demeanor began to shift to one of hopeful anticipation as his friend continued.

"Let's say that I considered... POSSIBLY..."

"Yeah?" Rin stared at Raz with eyes like wet saucers that got wider every second.

"...Sticking around?" Raz ventured cautiously. Rin couldn't contain himself any longer and burst into celebration. "Awwww... YEAAAAAH!!!" he yelled then leaped full force into Raz, wrapping him up in the biggest bear hug he'd felt in years.

"Ouch... my nuts," Raz squeaked.

When the air finally returned to his lungs, Raz took a deep breath, and gestured for a moment to recover.

"OK, big guy… We got about just over twenty four hours to come up with a plan. And I mean, we're gonna need something MAJOR. 'Cuz I've seen some kickin' ass in my time, and that back there was some of the most pathetic, tenth tier, last place in a cart race, discount bin, bottom of the barrel, 'kickin' ass', I've ever seen!"

"Well, I…" Rin's lips squeezed together tight in thought. Slowly, the rest of his face scrunched up like he'd just eaten a lemon, until he blew raspberries. "Yeah, we're gonna need a good plan."

Rin stared off, focusing all of his energy on the problem at hand. "One more day…" he said suddenly, echoing the words that had been repeating in Raz's head ever since he woke up. "That's plenty of time for us to put our heads together and figure out something better than volunteering to be Nox's punching bags."

It was true. They had a whole day. Raz had gotten

himself out of worse in less time. Maybe not worse, but pretty bad. Then, he looked over at Rin's dopey face. He wished he had better backup.

"I've got it!" Rin suddenly jumped up and began to pace beside the mattress like a general laying down a battle plan. "Shadowmaster Kito says that when you're stuck in a game you can't win, you've got to change the rules!"

"So..." Raz said cautiously, hoping to not seem like an idiot, "you're saying we should cheat?"

"Yeah! Actually, no. Not exactly. Kind of. But you said it yourself, we're no match for Nox in a straight fight. So, what if we could take down Nox without throwing a punch?"

"I'm listening," Raz replied cautiously. Rin twiddled his fingers deviously.

"You know how Master Klu's been all over the world right? Well, I heard he keeps a bunch of badass weapons under his dojo."

"That's it? That's all you got?" Raz deflated. This was already shaping up to be a disaster. "There's already weapons all over the monastery and Nox can use them ALL a whole lot better than us!"

"I don't mean regular weapons! I'm talking MAGICAL weapons! Stuff Master Klu probably collected from when he got mixed up in the Plague Wars!"

"Klu?!" Raz's ears pricked up. A big dope like Klu in the Plague Wars? That was the first he'd heard of it. "You sure we're talking about the same guy? There's no way a scatterbrain like him would be hoarding stuff like that."

"It's true! I snuck into the kitchen the other night after hours to grab a little snack, and overheard the other Masters complaining about how dangerous it all was."

"You snuck into the Celestial Temple after dark?! Past Tomo?"

Rin nodded casually, like it was the simplest thing in the world. Most kids who tried to pull a fast one on the monastery's custodian ended up mopping the floors or were put on gutter cleaning duty for months.

"How'd you manage that?!" Raz demanded. Rin took out the Ninja Arts Weekly and waved the cover in front of him as if it were an adequate explanation.

Raz started to take in the room and Rin in a whole new light. Was it really possible that a lummox like him snuck past the Masters undetected?

"If we could get into Klu's stash," Rin raved, now fully enveloped in his schemes, "we could find something that would teach Nox a lesson he'd never forget!"

Raz looked skeptical, "When you say magical, how magical are we talking here?"

"I mean the good stuff: scrolls, firebombs, ancient guardians, transformation spells, pocket dimensions, teleportation rings, exploding statues, you name it!" Rin said, his eyes twitching eagerly back and forth like the items were

laid out in front of him already.

"H-Hey, Nox is an ass but I don't want to," Raz gulped, "EXPLODE him! I don't think we'll be too popular around here if we kill the guy. We don't need to do anything more than give him a good hurtin'."

Rin paused, "Nox is all about his ego. We just need some kind of trick to beat him in a fight where everyone can see it. Then his whole reputation goes to pieces. He'd probably hide away for months, crying into his pillow!"

"Heck yeah!" Raz exclaimed. Suddenly, things were looking a lot more hopeful.

Rin looked at Raz expectantly. "Well? What do you say, partner?"

Partner, huh? Not sure if I like the sound of that, Raz thought, full of apprehension.

Raz scanned the room and gulped. "I guess…" Rin held his breath waiting for Raz to reply, "… I guess I'm in."

Rin froze then started twitching, shuffling along the floor with uncontained excitement. "Is this for real? Are we doing this? Are we ACTUALLY doing this?"

Raz took the most heroic stance he could muster without causing every muscle in his body to cry out in pain and nodded stoically. "It's either that or pack our bags. Let's do it!"

"YES! I knew you had it in ya!" Rin threw his fist into the air like he'd been waiting for this moment his whole life. "Don't worry, buddy, I won't let you down! I've got all kinds of tricks that you don't even know about!"

"I hope they're better than the 'tactical retreat' from before," Raz teased.

"Oh yeah, way better. Plus, I'm pretty good at patching you up after a fight. And considering that you seem to get your butt kicked all the time…"

"Alright, alright! No need to rub it in. Hey um..." Raz paused, lowering his voice a bit, "thanks for dragging me up here."

"Oh yeah. Don't mention it, that's what friends do!"

All this talk of friendship was making Raz uneasy. "Guess this makes us a team. For now," Raz added before extending his hand.   Rin gripped it and shook it violently, causing Raz's shoulder to seize up painfully. "Heck yeah! Team RiRaz!"

"Ooooooooowwwwwwww! Wait. What? Ri... Raz?" Raz interrupted, wrenching his stiff arm away.

"You know, RiRaz, like... you're Raz, and I'm —"

"No, I get it. Is that really what you want us to be known by after we defeat the Red Cobras and save Crescent Isle? Team RiRaz? Everyone will laugh at us! More than they already do..."

Rin thought on this for a second then shrugged. "We've got a whole day. Plenty of time to workshop it a bit."

Raz sighed and walked to one of the circular windows overlooking the market. Citizens happily walked around the large courtyard and raised walkways, oblivious to the high drama unfolding in the dumb-looking owl above the clothing shop.

A few Moonken students Raz didn't recognize ducked into Nico's bathhouse, and several others walked up to a fish and 'tater stand, spending their little allowances on a fried snack. There was no sign of Nox or the Cobras, but their presence could be felt everywhere. Merchants and townspeople nervously glanced at the innocent Moonken students, waiting for them to kick up trouble. The students who were there seemed cautious like they were watching their backs. It was Moonken like Nox that gave them all a bad name.

Soon, he'd have a chance to change all of that. One bully at a time.

"Well, no use standing around waiting," Raz said. "What's our next move?"

Rin thought and stroked his chin. He slapped a fist into his palm decisively. He ran off and rummaged around in the far corner of the room, returning moments later with a jar of yellow cream which he shoved into Raz's hands.

"Rub this on yourself!" he ordered.

Raz sniffed it and wretched. "Ugh, it stinks! What is this crap? Spoiled milk?"

"Quit whining! Secret ninja recipe! It'll help you heal faster," Rin explained. He picked up a pack and threw a grappling hook made of sharpened coat hooks into it. "If we're gonna do this, I need you in tip top shape!"

"Augh! Do this when exactly?"

Rin picked up a handful of ninja stars and threw them into his pack before turning to Raz with a smile.

"Tonight. Operation: Cobra Spank commences in one hour."

Raz groaned. "Hey, I uh…. I think we're need to workshop that name, too."

It's a Secret To Everyone

Crescent Isle has not always been a bustling market for trading and potato farming. Long before the many merchants and trevelers from all over Speria settled into the relatively small island, it was home only to the Ancient Monks of Twilight.

A thousand years ago, the Ancients disappeared, their story drifted into legend and myth. The island appeared to be abandoned and forgotten. 800 years passed before the Moonken would begin to reclaim their history.

Even the current Masters of the Celestial Temple do not know the purpose of the mysterious tunnels beneath the island, The many chambers, vaults, and coridoors contain ancient history that even the ethereal Master Kozomo cannot see.

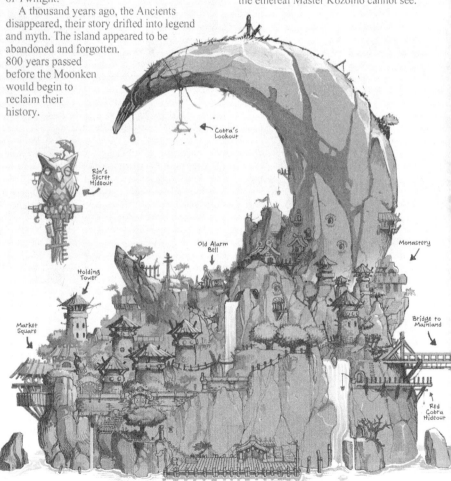

Cobra's Lookout

Rin's Secret Hideout

Old Alarm Bell

Monastery

Holding Tower

Market Square

Bridge to Mainland

Red Cobra Hideout

CHAPTER 3
IN THE SHADOW OF TITANS

Ocean water erupted off the stones and into Raz's face, causing him to nearly slip and plummet to his death along the hundred-foot cliff wall on the backside of Crescent Isle. He swore under his breath, trying to keep up with Rin, who nimbly jumped between the slick stones of the Monk's Path like he'd done it a thousand times before. The big Moonken's feet fell on the wet stones like feathers; his grey robes blended seamlessly into the surroundings.

What a show-off, Raz thought, as he carefully picked his way along the stones, heavy footsteps slapping on the rocks like a wet fish. Taking a chance to steady his nerves, Raz looked out over the sea to the two lonely spires of rock that held Klu's Dojo and its grounds. It didn't look any closer. He hoped it was his imagination.

Of course, any sane person would have lowered the drawbridge to get to Klu's Dojo. The bridge had been explicitly built so that people didn't fall and die taking the old Monk's Path – the bridge that even Master Dou, the leader of the Celestial Temple, took regularly.

Sure, lowering it in the middle of the night so they could swipe a few magical items from an old Master was not precisely low-key. In Rin's words, it would jeopardize the mission. But taking the old path half blind in the middle of the night was just about hardcore enough practice for a guy like Rin.

This was suicide. And Rin was loving every second of it. Stealth operations were his specialty. He was surprisingly agile as long as he didn't have to fight.

Nervously, Raz traced further along the path with his eyes. It got thinner; each jump more spread out than the last. Every step provided a new and grotesque way to fall and break into a million bloody pieces.

Fifty feet ahead, Rin waved his arms impatiently for Raz to hurry up. Raz grunted and slowly inched forward.

Perched on a thin sliver of rock, Rin tapped at an imaginary watch, smiling stupidly as Raz got closer.

"You don't have to sit there waiting for me. I can figure it out myself," Raz mumbled, looking out over the edge nervously.

"Huh?" Rin strained to hear Raz over the wind and waves then followed his gaze to the ocean. "Hey, don't worry about it. It's okay if you're afraid of heights!" he gestured encouragingly.

Raz's jaw clamped shut. He flapped his arms to his side. "I already told you, I am not —"

"You know, that reminds me of something…" Rin trailed off and rummaged in his bag.

Raz's eye twitched. He reckoned he knew what was

coming next. A pattern had established itself ever since Rin had revealed his little secret the night before. The floodgates of his mind were open, and he couldn't stop yapping about every secret ninja trick he'd ever learned. If Raz had to hear any more words of wisdom from Shadowmaster Kito, he might lose it.

"Shadowmaster Kito says," Rin began, taking a Ninja Arts Weekly out of his bag, "that you should embrace your fears as an ally."

There it was. It was unclear how many of these nuggets of wisdom he carried with him on an average day. One was already too many. Rin kept going on, ignoring the furnace of frustration in front of him.

"Only by embracing your fears totally can you —" Quickly, Raz jumped up and snatched the magazine from Rin's hands.

"Yeah?! Well, what does Master Kito say about THIS?!"

Raz hurled the magazine off the edge. Smug satisfaction quickly changed to abject terror as his planted leg slipped and gave way beneath him. Before he could figure out what was happening, he was already making the horrifying slide over the edge. Just as he was about to crest the side of the cliff and fall, a hand grasped his wrist.

Rin held him tight, his upper body hanging over the edge, his feet hooked into some hidden crevice of the rock. He pulled Raz back onto solid ground and cleared his throat, "Ahem! As I was saying, only by embracing your fears totally can you conquer them."

"That was a heck of a catch," Raz murmured.

"I was aiming for the magazine," Rin replied then laughed. "I'm joking. I'm joking! I couldn't let my bestest pal fall to his death. What kinda friend would I be? Plus, I've got like... four copies of that one stored away back in the command center."

"Command center? You mean the owl?" Raz asked while he rubbed at his side, the one he'd just slammed into the rock. That was another bruise he'd taken for this guy. He doubted it would be the last. It was bad enough that Rin kept miraculously avoiding injury, but all the smiling and joking all the time made it worse. Raz just couldn't figure him out.

"Hmmm... you're right," Rin mused, oblivious to Raz's discomfort. "It should have a cooler name. Anyway, guess saving your life just now with that catch makes us even?"

Yeah, Even-Steven, Raz thought to himself. Except that he wouldn't have even been there if it weren't for him.

"Come on, let's get going," Raz grunted in reply.

Hopping from stone to stone, they eventually passed under several ancient, dilapidated archways and came at last to the two large flat sea stacks that held the Dojo and its grounds. The two rocks were connected to each other with a rickety wooden bridge. In striking contrast to the bare stones of the path, the dojo grounds were wide and lush with vegetation, covered in long green grass and dotted with mossy stones.

They stepped onto the soft grass, releasing a wave of fireflies into the air around them. Despite the wind and the surrounding sea, there was a profound stillness here. The old Dojo felt like a place out of time, refusing to change in the face of the quick pace of modern life. The peace and silence made Raz's mind drift through dusty memories of places long forgotten, and the people and other things he'd lost along the way.

"Pssst!" Rin called out, hands cupped over his mouth. He had already taken up a position next to the bridge behind a large rock. Suddenly conscious that he was exposed, Raz hustled over and crouched next to Rin. Slowly, they peeked their heads around the corner to look over the bridge at Klu's Dojo.

Despite its impressive history, the Dojo itself appeared nothing more than an oversized shack of two stories. It was made of ancient wood with the odd rotting board here and there. Any paint that had once covered it was all but gone, the original colors left to the imagination. These days it didn't get much use and remained mostly empty. Except for Master Klu, that is.

On the second floor was a wide paper window, spattered with holes. Candlelight cast the lanky shadow of Master Klu onto the window in full. His erratic and swaying movements oddly in sync with the random sputtering of the candlelight. The blurry shadow moved across the window in strange arcs, seemingly without reason and in no hurry. The old Moonken's unkempt hair looked in silhouette like a rough, woolen cloud. Klu's shadow shrunk as he approached the window. Like a bending stalk of grass, he bent to the side and extended his arm out of frame. Raz could just hear the scratch of a needle on a record player. Music, or some sort of approximation of music, started to play.

"Well, go on master ninja. You're the sneaking expert. What do we do now?" Raz whispered to Rin. Casually, Rin withdrew a sandwich from his belt and began to munch on it.

"Lff lrrfff olrff mnnfffsh schtll awrrrr," he mumbled through bites of ham and cheese. Raz pointed to his ear and shrugged his shoulders.

Rin swallowed loudly. "Looks like the old man's still awake," he said again and picked at his teeth.

"Wow. Good thing you're here to tell me that," Raz replied flatly.

"Let's hold back for a bit. Look, we can stay out of sight over there!" He pointed to a clearing surrounded by mossy stones about forty feet away. Like an animal on the prowl, Rin slumped down on all fours and crawled away through the tall grass.

Cautiously, Raz peered around the corner at the Dojo again one last time and suddenly felt very silly. Afterall, Klu was harmless.

He trotted after Rin and called out to him, trying his best to keep his voice down. "You know, Klu's not so bad. He's not a tight ass like the other Masters. He might even help us."

Raz was pulled down into the grass with a violent yank, so he was face to face with Rin. "Nope. No way," Rin said flatly and took another bite of his sandwich. "Are you suggesting we walk up, knock on the front door and ask, 'Hey Master Klu, can we borrow some of your hidden ancient magical weapons please?'"

"Well…" Raz scratched the back of his head and averted his gaze. It didn't sound so good coming out of someone else's mouth.

"Don't be ridiculous. Klu is chill, but he's not that chill."

"But—"

"He was in the Plague Wars, Raz, the PLAGUE WARS!"

"Klu? I mean, you said that before but you don't actually believe that, do you?"

Raz glanced up, but Rin was no longer looking at him. He peered out over Raz's shoulder toward the window as if the old scatterbrain might jump out, weapons drawn, at any minute. Raz sighed and rolled his eyes.

"Fine. We do it your way."

Rin breathed a sigh of relief and fished his hand into his bag again and pulled out another sandwich. "You hungry?"

Raz shook his head and popped up over the grass, peering at the Dojo again. The shadow of Klu swayed in odd rhythm to the music like a tree blown in the wind.

"Besides," Rin grinned, pulling out some rope and a small lock picking kit from the sleeves of his robes, "I didn't bring all this stuff for nothin'!"

They passed into the clearing, which appeared to be the remnants of an ancient courtyard. Surrounding them were several tall, moss-covered stones of unusual and varied shape, with a thick layer of overgrowth growing in the gaps between them. It would serve to keep them out of sight just fine until Klu fell asleep.

In the center of the space was a single stone pedestal that Raz first mistook for a fountain. There was no basin on it, only a flat surface on which a single person could sit quietly. Very monk-like.

Idly, Raz kicked at a pebble, occasionally glancing through the overgrowth towards the light from Klu's room. The shadow still moved erratically against the paper screen. Impatiently, Raz kicked the pebble harder, sending it ricocheting off of a strange protrusion in the rock. Then he paused. The rock looked strangely fist-like.

The moonlight broke through the clouds and cast a clear white light that revealed the rocks to be not mere rocks, but statues. Now illuminated, he could make out faces, clothes, and weapons. Their features and the long, pointed ears were unmistakably Moonken.

"The Monks of Twilight," Rin mused. He rose and stood next to Raz to admire the ancient figures. Many of the faces were so old and weathered that they were barely distinguishable anymore.   Raz looked around him and realized that all the rocks on the dojo grounds might have been statues like these at one point. Weather and time had taken their toll - the Twilight Monks had been forgotten, even by the Masters.

They walked along the base of the statues admiringly. Rin pointed out the ones he knew, naming them off one by one. "Anako... Typhon, I think? And there's Malifera and Yuga...."

No one knew how many Twilight Monks there were for sure, only that they were once the most powerful beings in Speria - heroes of a forgotten age.

Rin came to a stop beneath one that weather had turned into little more than a large, lump. The face was mostly worn away. It was posed, in such a fashion as if it were meant to hold some sort of weapon, which had broken away long ago.

"Hey, it's Torra! That's me!" he said, rubbing the statue's weathered base.

Until that point, it never occurred to Raz to ask which constellation Rin was born from. It was a sensitive topic for their kind. When a newborn Moonken fell to Speria, people usually didn't see it as a happy occasion. Most Moonken learned their origin names in the hushed whispers of people who feared them. They were called other things, too: creatures from the stars, harbingers of chaos, pointy-eared monsters. Freaks. Some like Rin got lucky, found by Earthparents compassionate enough to take them and

give them a new name. But all Earthparents, no matter how loving, knew Moonken weren't like them. They all took them to Crescent Isle, eventually. However, not every Moonken who fell to Speria made it to the island. Some didn't make it at all.

"Rin Torra, huh?" Raz remarked.

Rin beamed with pride. "That's right! Y'know, those born of Torra are meant to be fearsome warriors," he said, waggling his eyebrows.

Raz cracked up. "A warrior? You? I dunno man, you sure you're a Torra?"

"What's so funny? Don't you think I'm... FIERCE?!" Rin responded, curling his hands into claws and growling like a tiger. Then, he too broke into a giggle.

Raz stared up at the Torra statue, or what was left of it, and frowned. "How can you tell it's Torra, anyway?" he asked.

Rin smiled and nodded to the sea of stars above. "See him up there? Torra, the sign of the tiger," he said as he traced the shape in the sky with his finger. "Those three dots there represent the tail."

Raz squinted up at the stars and eventually found Torra's constellation. "Yeah? So what?"

"Look here," Rin continued and waved for Raz to come closer. He pointed to a series of circles and lines carved into the base of the statue - the constellation of Torra.

"Hmmm, I wonder…" Raz mumbled and started pacing around the circle of statues again. Finally, he found the one he was looking for and studied it. The face held a serene expression despite being posed for battle. The figure was lean and held one clenched fist in front of it, with another open palm near its face.

Rin crouched down next to Raz and squinted to make out the constellation. "Tenza? You never told me you were a Tenza," Rin said, with a hint of awe in his voice.

Raz looked up with wonder at the face of Tenza, the Twilight Monk that bore his namesake. He'd never actually seen him depicted before.

"Yup, that's me," Raz said, patting the statue. "Alright, so what's my deal then? Torras are warriors, or whatever, so what are Tenzas known for?"

Rin stood up, rigid and stiff, his face went cold and his eyes went wide. "Hold on. You're a Tenza!" Rin exclaimed as if realizing it for the first time.

"Yeah?"

"Don't you realize what this means?!"

"I eat people?" Raz replied sarcastically.

"No! It means we were brought together by fate!"

"I think we were brought together by Tomo when he assigned me to your room," Raz countered, raising his eyebrows.

Rin flopped onto his back, and patted the space next to him. Raz sighed heavily and laid down on the overgrown stones, folding his hands on his stomach and staring up at the sky above.

"See there's Torra, and WAY over there... that's Tenza," Rin said, tracing a line across the sky. Raz found Tenza and frowned.
"Tenza always looks... dimmer than the others," he complained.

"It's said that Tenza, is the 'Wanderer'," Rin explained with an air of mystery in his voice. "Pretty badass, if you ask me."

"The wanderer, huh? Seems about right," Raz mumbled. "Still, I don't get it. What's your point?"

"Check it out! There are Torra and Tenza. And that one there is Anako, the owl. Then that one with the three points is Typhon," he continued, moving his arm in a big sweeping counterclockwise circle as he pointed to each constellation. "There's Kani. And then, BOOM! See that one Raz?"

"Which one?" Raz sputtered, snapping back to attention on hearing his name. This all seemed like more of the Master's mystical mumbo jumbo to him.

"Uhhh… the one that kinda looks like a crab?"

"Heh, it does, doesn't it? But you're wrong. That's Yuga, the bull."

"Those ancients must have been smoking something. How is that a bull?" Raz quipped.

"Beats me! But it's a bull!" Rin replied enthusiastically. "I promise you that!"

"You know, you still haven't gotten to the point," Raz droned.

"Patience, my young ninja-in-training," Rin cooed and then returned his attention to the heavens. "The different Moonken signs all make a big circle in the sky. The Masters say that the ones that are across from each other are cosmic pairs, eternally balancing out each other's energies. See how Anako balances out Typhon across the circle? And Kani balances Yuga?"

Raz traced his eyes around the circle of constellations then grimaced.

"Let me guess. Torra and Tenza…"

"... Are COSMIC PAIRS, buddy!" Rin said with much enthusiasm.

Raz sighed. "Oh, goody. So what's that mean, exactly?"

Rin scratched at his chin. "Hmmm, I'm not entirely sure. BUT, it definitely means that Team RiRaz is destined for greatness."

Raz said nothing and rose to sit on the pedestal in the middle of the clearing. Even with his eyes closed, he could feel the eyes of the stone Monks of Twilight on him.

"Ever wonder how much of those old legends are true?" Raz asked, eyes still closed. "You know, about the Monks of Twilight. They were supposed to be the ultimate badass Darksprite demon hunters, right? I wish they were still around."

"Master Yobei says the Monks of Twilight disappeared a thousand years ago, after the war with the Darksprites or some such," Rin mused. "He says that's what shattered the Sperian Earthshells, I think. Some sort of big cataclysmic fight to end all fights."

"It's weird, though, right? These crazy powerful Moonken fight the evil demons, save the world, and now people barely talk about them," Raz noted, keeping his eyes closed as daydreams of supremely powerful Moonken whistled past in his mind's eye.

"Hmmm… you got me there. It seems like if they were really that powerful, they wouldn't have been forgotten. I mean, some people don't even think they were real," Rin mused.

"They HAD to have been real," Raz burst out suddenly. "They were heroes. If it weren't for the Monks of Twilight, the Darksprites would have taken over Speria."

"Moonken heroes…" Rin repeated, his eyes swimming in a daydream. "Not exactly the first thing people think of when they say 'Moonken', is it?"

"Nope. If you ask me, the Moonken Masters nowadays

are a pretty far cry from all of that. I bet the Twilight Monks didn't just sit around meditating every time someone in Speria was trouble." He looked up at the statue, admiring its presence. "If there was a problem, WHAM!" He slammed a fist into his open palm. "I bet they'd put a stop to it right there and then! It didn't matter if it was Darksprites, evil necrotic dragons, or even highway bandits."

A subtle smile wormed its way onto Rin's face at Raz's sudden outburst. "I didn't know you were so passionate about the ancients."

Raz snorted, ignoring the comment. "What would you do if you had that kind of power?" Raz thought aloud.

"What? Like the Monks of Twilight?" Rin wrinkled his forehead as he considered it. "I dunno. Guess I never really thought about it," he replied honestly. "You?"

"If I had their power, I'd even out the scales. Let the little guy win for a change."

"Not a bad idea. But then again, if the ancient Moonken were so powerful that they could break Speria itself, it's no wonder people are still so afraid of us now."

Raz's eye cracked open a hair, and he saw Rin unconsciously raise a hand to his forehead where the scar was hidden.

No one said anything for a time. Still, there was a profound sense of power in that small clearing, a sense that change could be enacted in the world. Crescent Isle, if legends were to be believed, was left behind by the Twilight Monks themselves. Sure, it was crumbling apart, and it's not much more than a rest stop for tourists, but still, there really was something special about hidden places like the one they were in. Being a Moonken was often more of a curse than a blessing, but surrounded by those statues, Raz didn't feel ashamed of what he was for once. In fact, listening to Rin talk about it, he almost felt proud to be a Moonken.

Raz's thoughts were broken when Klu's strange music

abruptly stopped. He looked across to the Dojo and saw the light on the second floor was out.

The two looked at each other, nodded, and stood at once. Rin gathered his things, and they began to move back through the grass towards the bridge. Raz glanced over his shoulder one last time at the old weathered statues.

The Monks of Twilight, the legendary heroes of the past, were nothing more than forgotten statues now.

An inch at a time, they crawled towards the bridge, keeping their eyes peeled on the Dojo. It was dark and still, no signs of the old Master. Raz exchanged a glance with Rin then slowly took the first step onto the bridge. Soon, Rin was at his side, holding a lockpick in his hand and smiling like it was his birthday.

"Come on, buddy. Time to find us a hidden stash."

CHAPTER 4

THE MESSY MASTER

Ten minutes. Ten tedious, agonizing minutes had passed, and Rin was no closer to picking the lock. The same kid who claimed to sneak into the monastery after dark like it was child's play couldn't get through a door that looked so old it would probably crumble of its own accord in a stiff breeze. Sickenly, as he watched Rin fumble with the lock pick yet again, Raz wondered if his confidence was misplaced, if the whole mission he'd staked his future on was founded on any truth at all.

Rin glanced over and saw Raz staring daggers at him. He shifted uncomfortably and returned his eyes to his task.

"So…' Beast of Tuksa'," he said casually, keeping his voice low. "Far as nicknames go, that one's pretty unique. Better than 'fatty', anyway."

Raz grimaced. "It's just a stupid name. Doesn't mean anything. Nothing that happened before means anything. You know that."

Rin nodded as if he understood, but then he opened his mouth to say more and proved that he did not. "That's not what I heard... how is it that a Moonken as old as you can show up outta nowhere and get a name like that? C'mon! You've gotta tell me! I bet there's a crazy story behind it."

"Yeah," Raz replied curtly, rubbing the wound in his shoulder. A reminder of some horrible beast that had nearly taken his life long ago. Rin stopped fiddling with the tools, eager to hear more.

But Raz turned away. "Not one I wanna talk about."

Rin sighed quietly with disappointment then reluctantly got back to work, sticking his tongue out in concentration.

"Just get the damn door open and drop the chit chat, will ya?"

Rin's eyes bounced back and forth from the lock to Raz, making it obvious that it wasn't going to happen. "I heard some of the other Moonken talking about it and they-"

Raz quickly cut him off, "They don't know the first thing about it. Or me. Whatever they said isn't true. End of story."

"Something about a cursed forest...?" Rin obliviously continued.

"Hey! Drop it," Raz ordered definitively. Thankfully, this time it seemed Rin finally would.

Raz nervously scanned the area around the dojo's entrance. He'd been here before plenty of times, but now he found himself jumping at every shadow cast by a bush or tree. Part of him was excited, he couldn't deny, but mostly he just wanted Rin to hurry the heck up. "Come on Rin, at this rate the sun's gonna be up by the time you get in there!" Raz hissed impatiently.

TWINK!

The lock pick snapped in half and twirled away into the bushes. Raz's eye twitched neurotically.

"Whoops," Rin mumbled absentmindedly. "Let's see..."

It didn't matter if they got caught. Raz couldn't take another second of Rin's buffoonery. He stormed forward, grabbed Rin by the shoulders, and moved him aside.

"Move!" Raz ordered and studied the door. "Lemme have a look."

Without thinking, he tried the latch and...

...*Click.*

Raz's face went completely blank. He turned back to Rin and without breaking eye contact, gave the door the gentlest of pushes. It slid open with no resistance. Unlocked. THE ENTIRE TIME!   After a moment of stunned silence, Rin quickly packed up his tools.

"Heh...heh heh," he laughed nervously. "Guess that's why I couldn't get the stupid lock to turn over... "He flicked at the open lock. "Ya know, these older model locks are complic -"

Raz rolled his eyes. "Forget it. Let's just go already," he said.

The two crept through the entrance. One of the older wooden boards creaked underfoot. They held their breath, standing still like statues. Above them, a flute played a lazy melody.

"Crap! He's awake!" Raz whispered.

The notes of the flute were soon replaced by a much louder and more vocal noise. Their muscles tensed, ready to run at any second. Then, the flute started up again, playing the same relaxed melody as if no interruption had taken place.

"Is he...?" Raz wondered aloud and Rin nodded in agreement. "No way..." They stopped talking and listened to the repetition of noises again.

"He's playing in his sleep," Rin confirmed in wonderment.

The rhythmic interchange of music and snoring continued at regular intervals. A giggle got caught in Raz's throat, but Rin gave him a harsh look and shoved a finger to his lips.

That's right - stealing from Master Klu, the secret mission, certain exile and probably death if I laugh. Got it.

He stayed silent.

They passed through the first-floor training room, inappropriately named perhaps, as very little martial training ever actually took place there. More often than not, instead of sparring, Master Klu would open the doors out to the sea and instructed meditation and posed thought puzzles. Training weapons gathered dust; the massive dojo smelled more heavily of incense than of sweat or blood. Such was the way of things under the freewheeling sensibilities of Master Klu.

An odd choice to lead the dojo, Master Klu was the least martially impressive of all the Masters. Most students in the monastery considered Klu eccentric and difficult. He was a man who rode the winds, thoughts flitting from one thing to the next, unconcerned with the petty trials and tribulations of the day-to-day.   There was a relaxed, laid back energy that radiated from him. As a result, Raz found he could relax around him. Klu wasn't quite as stringent as the other Masters, not as critical of every little thing, and seemed to go wherever the universe took him. At any given moment, he simply was where he was at this time in his life. He was gentle and trusting.

Raz liked him, and he was betraying that trust. He couldn't help but feel a little guilty.

Raz looked around the room. There was nothing here they hadn't seen a hundred times before in the daytime. This whole thing was starting to feel like a wild goose chase.

"Well, braniac, where's the secret stash?" he whispered to his partner in crime.

Balancing on one leg, Rin slowly spun in a circle like a human dowsing rod until he finally came to a stop, pointing towards a door at the back of the room.

"That's just the storage space. Even I know that," Raz said.

"Yup," Rin nodded. "And that's where we're gonna start our search. Remember Shadowmaster Kito? Key to stealth is to hide in plain sight, remember?"

Rooms are often named on blueprints for their planned use, but it was highly doubtful that the dojo's storage room was originally intended to be a storage room. Inside, they were confronted with piles upon piles of assorted objects cluttering every inch of free space and stacked as high as the ceiling. Raz scanned the various scrolls with odd symbols, stuffed bananas, boxing gloves, knick-knacks, old photos, postcards, and wooden fighting dummies. And that was only the contents of the closest pile.

Careful not to disturb anything, they stepped into the room and closed the door behind them. Raz's eyes met Rin's, begging him for any sort of direction. Rin merely shrugged and started rummaging through the piles. With a sinking feeling in his chest, Raz had no choice but to do the same.

Raz began to feel a little sick as he realized that he was going to leave this place with nothing but knick-knacks to fight Nox with. It was all the kind of useless garbage anyone might pick up on the road: maps, scrolls, and novelties intermixed with training gear and old clothes.

"Is this it?" Raz hissed, trying to keep the panic out of his voice.

"Huh? Naw, man. The Masters said Klu's collection was dangerous! Does this stuff look dangerous to you? There's probably a hidden room or something. Just keep looking," came Rin's reply from behind a stack of souvenir shirts the size of a tall man.

Raz sighed and rifled through a stack of novelty

postcards, and poked a few snowglobes.

"Hidden stash, he says, it'll be cool, he says," Raz grumbled bitterly under his breath, "See what happens when you don't follow your gut, Tenza?"

Raz froze as he heard a strange, clunking shuffle behind him. Had they been too loud? Had they awakened the old master?

Slowly he turned and saw a foot. It was dressed in full battle armor.

Crap.

Slowly, his eyes glanced upward as the figure lumbered into the light. First, he saw hardened leather shin guards and a skirt of woven leather protecting the thighs, then a breastplate with a golden tiger embroidered into it.

Crap, crap, crap...

Finally, with much trepidation, he looked at the face.

Rin beamed back at him beneath a spiked metal helmet one size too small for his bulbous head.

"Are you freakin' serio--" Raz wound up, ready to let Rin have it.

"Shhhh! You wanna wake up the old man?" he demanded, adjusting the helmet on his head.

"If we're gonna find that stash, you gotta take the mission seriously!" Raz stammered out a few questioning babbles, but did not manage to formulate a coherent sentence. Rin assumed Raz's lack of words was on account of the armor.

"Pretty cool, right? Can you believe Klu just had this lying around?"

"How is that going to help us?!"

"Hmmmm… If we can't find Klu's secret stash, we could always wear these around and reduce the damage?"

Taking one last look to confirm once and for all that this room was filled with nothing but useless trinkets, he charged Rin, stopping just short of his face.

"Is this why you brought me here?" he demanded at last, his voice breaking above a whisper. They both froze, nervously eyeing the ceiling and listening for Klu. After a few moments, they breathed a sigh of relief as Klu's loud snoring continued. Raz gestured apologetically and lowered his voice.

"Are we only here so you can mess around with the stuff in this storeroom? Tell me the truth," he accused.

"Huh? No, of course not!" Rin protested innocently.

"Then where's all the magical stuff? I don't think this," Raz said, signaling to roughly the entirety of Rin's armor-clad body, "would scare an old lady, and it definitely won't scare Nox!"

"I don't know! I'm looking!"

Raz fumed and scanned the room. "Are you sure you heard the Masters right? Are you sure they didn't think it was dangerous because all of this crap is a fire hazard or something?"

Rin lowered his head. "They said there were terrible and dangerous artifacts here! I swear!"

Raz picked up a rubber chicken, tossed it up into the air and caught it. "Yeah, they're terrible, all right."

The chicken bounced off Rin's helmet with a squeak. Something caught Raz's eye. He rushed to hold Rin's helmet in place before the big guy could adjust it.

"What?" Rin nervously darted his eyes from side to side. "Is there something on my face?"

There was. More specifically, there was a tiny point of light reflected off the metal, too bright to be the diffused moonlight from the windows. With one hand, Raz held Rin's head in place and carefully turned it this way and that to make sure it wasn't a trick of the light. He followed its source to a single pinprick coming from a space in the wall next to a large novelty fish mounted on the wall. The fish had a little mustache, monocle, and top hat. Classy.

"What is THAT?"

"It's a Funky Fish," Rin replied behind him, "they were all the rage on Crescent Isle a few years ago. People used to collect 'em."

Raz sighed. "Not that! THAT!" he said again and pointed at the light.

"Oh. Right. Sorry."

Raz got his face right up close to it and tried to look through. He could feel a cold wind on his face. "There's something back there," he observed. Rin grinned and pushed in behind him, bulkier than usual thanks to the armor.

"See? I told you! That there is a bonafide hidden compartment! Klu's stash here we come!"

"Maybe. Won't know until we move it. Give me a hand."

The two took up positions on either side of the fish and

tugged at the wooden board it was attached to, but it didn't budge. Several times, they pushed and pulled it at various angles, but all to the same result. They checked for screws or some sort of mounting hooks but found nothing. It's like the Funky Fish grew from the wall itself. It mocked their futile efforts with a fixed, upper-class grin.

"Dammit! We're so close! Why won't it move?" Raz panted. He scanned the room then strode over to a weapon rack and grabbed a broad sword. He came back, looked at the hole the light was coming from, and was about to shove the point in to try and lever it open when Rin waved his arms frantically.

"Stop! You'll wake up the whole damn island if you do that!"

"Do you have a better idea?" Raz growled.

"Hmmmm…" Rin stripped off the armor reluctantly and put it neatly on the floor. He approached the fish, contemplating its many mysteries. "Who do you think makes those tiny little hats?" he asked aloud.

"Rin!" Raz pleaded.

"I know, I know! I'm thinking!" After contemplating the gaudy fish for a moment, he slid two fingers in behind the mounting board, moving them slowly along the base.

"We already looked for screws, remember?"

Rin shushed him, and got back to his task, fully concentrating on whatever it was he was doing. Raz worried this would be a repeat of the front door lock all over again.

CLICK!

With that, the fish did a little fin flap, and the board and a section of the wall about three feet wide swung open. Rin stepped back and placed his hands on his hips, admiring his handiwork. Raz stood in awe; another mystery laid bare before him. It felt like he'd accomplished more in the last few hours than months of strict training.

Rin announced proudly, "Ninja Arts Magazine, issue

number twenty-two: the history edition. The Higa Clan used to put hidden switches on their art to conceal secret escape passages for when they were attacked,". It was clear that he savored his moment of triumph.

They looked on for a moment and admired the sheer audacity of a passage hidden behind a novelty fish. Leave it to Klu to hide his greatest treasure behind the most ridiculous item in his collection. In hindsight, it felt so obvious, given his personality.   Finally, Rin broke the silence and, with a cordial gesture beckoned Raz forward. "Shall we?"

The two Moonken entered the small corridor. The source of the light turned out to be a small glowing stone, but beyond it there was only darkness. Having found what they were truly searching for, and perhaps only half expecting to find it, they both found themselves feeling tremendously out of their depth. Neither of them, of course, would admit that. They cautiously proceeded, eventually reaching narrow wooden stairs that wound down in a great spiral into the inky blackness.

The stairs went on for far longer than either of them had anticipated, and they surmised that they must be deep within the spire that held the dojo itself. In the dark, they moved slowly and cautiously, the only light source now from a small glowing stone Rin held out in front of him. Their slow progress made it hard to tell exactly how far down they were, but the air quality itself changed.

Raz jumped in surprise when his foot hit the bottom of the staircase. It didn't take long before they hit a dead end. Only, it wasn't just any dead end.

"You seeing what I'm seeing?" Rin asked.

"If you are too, then I think we both might be going nuts," Raz replied.

In front of them was the bark of an ancient oak tree, underground, fused so seamlessly with the stone wall that it

was as though the rocks were growing around the tree itself.
Glimmering gold patterns traced themselves up the bark and
into branches, which extended into the wall and out of sight.
In the middle of the wall were two golden nobs, as if the tree
itself were some kind of door, but Raz could see no indication
of how it might open.

"Anything in Ninja Arts Weekly about glowing
underground tree doors?" Raz teased.

Rin scratched his head as he ran his hand along with
the bark in vain for some sort of seam or switch. "Negative,
buddy. This is some genuine mysterious master of Kung
Fulio magic here."

Raz took a step back to observe the door in its entirety.
Several dim glimmers that lined the branches caught his eye.

"Hey Rin, put away that light for a sec."

Rin obediently shoved the light into his pocket. As soon as he did, the golden patterns on the door sprang to life in their entirety. Centered above the two golden knobs was the symbol of the Moonken, an open semi-circle with a small dot in it. The emblem was dotted all across Crescent Isle, especially on its oldest structures. The lack of artificial light also revealed two golden handprints between the golden knobs.

"Nice one!" Rin said excitedly and patted Raz on the back.

Feels good to be solving problems for a change, Raz thought and smiled. "Two right hands," Raz observed. "Unless you've got a mutation I never noticed, we'd better do this together."

Simultaneously, they placed their hands on the golden handprints. The tree reacted instantly as a pulse of light emanated from the Moonken symbol. A line of golden energy sliced its way up the center of the bark, revealing a seam. The tree creaked and moaned as the newly formed door opened inward on its own accord. One at a time, they moved into the narrow opening into the space beyond.

Above them, the light from the door began to spread, igniting a vast canopy of leaves in a magical golden light. The light from the impossible tree revealed a massive space. As it did the young Moonken found themselves stupefied, their heads rapidly darting back and forth, unable to focus on one single point. Silently, Rin held up a fist, and Raz bumped it with his.

No more knick-knacks and novelties. They'd hit the jackpot.

CHAPTER 5
MASTER KLU'S STASH

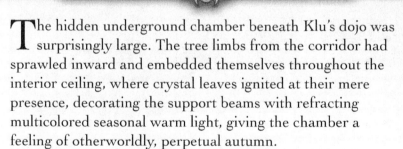

The hidden underground chamber beneath Klu's dojo was surprisingly large. The tree limbs from the corridor had sprawled inward and embedded themselves throughout the interior ceiling, where crystal leaves ignited at their mere presence, decorating the support beams with refracting multicolored seasonal warm light, giving the chamber a feeling of otherworldly, perpetual autumn.

The three bookshelves contained hundreds of tomes. They set in a row along the back wall. Neatly arranged urns had been stuffed with gems of all sizes, that glowed brighter than the peaches of Giant's Crown. A number of ornate weapons adorned the right wall, and a series of elegantly patterned porcelain cylinders had been organized and stacked side-by-side around the perimeter of the room.

Raz perused the various glowing objects on the shelves,

enthralled.

He shook the small glass jar in his hand again and listened as the sharp, oddly angular rock gently tinkled against the glass and glowed a dull purple. The jar was one of dozens just like it. This shelf was labeled 'Star Crystals'. Beneath it was a little handwritten sign that read: 'Do not disturb or risk possible cosmic terror'. Raz shook the jar again.

"Oh. My. God," Rin gasped breathlessly, from across the room. "I didn't even know these existed in real life! Am I dreaming right now? This must be a dream."

Raz grabbed a different jar suspecting the first might be defective. The small emerald inside wiggled around as soon as he touched the glass. He raised it up to his face and gave it a rough shake. A vertical slit opened on the gem's surface into a single eye with two irises, staring angrily at him. He flinched and shoved it back onto the shelf. The crystal inside vibrated, causing the others on the shelf to wiggle in their jars as well.

Okay... guess we won't be using Star Crystals to take down Nox then, Raz thought, turning away slowly to avoid making eye contact with the… unsettling rock. He found Rin waiting immediately behind him, stamping up and down on his feet like an excited child.

"Raz, Raz, Raz, Raz..." he repeated again and again, waiting eagerly for a response.

"WHAT?!" Raz demanded. After what seemed like an hour of searching, or getting their bearings, Rin's enthusiasm hadn't dropped in the slightest.

"Do you SEE what I'm holding right now?" Rin said and held out a small purple bag.

"Yeah…? What is it?" Raz asked, squinting at the small pouch.

"It's size dust, man! Do you have any idea how rare this

stuff is?"

"No, but I'm assuming it uh… changes your size?" Raz ventured. Rin nodded excitedly, holding the bag up in front of him with both hands. "Think about it! Nox can't fight us if he's the size of an ant! It's perfect!"

"Heh, maybe we could drop him in a hornet's nest and make him contemplate his life choices," Raz mused with a smile, which disappeared moments later. "Wait, but it's size dust, right? Doesn't say which size. What if it makes him… bigger?"

Rin frowned at the purple bag in his hands. "Huh, didn't really think about that. Guess this one's a no-go too then, huh?" He gingerly put it back on the shelf. The wrong shelf.

Raz knew it was the wrong shelf because, unlike the bomb site of unneeded junk in the dojo above, everything, absolutely everything, in Klu's stash was meticulously organized. Spells and incantations, poisons and potions, pocket dimensions and spirit wire, and all things Raz had never even heard of before were staged neatly. Paper tags detailing names and places of origin were attached to every item.

The tall shelves were curved, arranged in concentric semi-circles, creating a maze of powerful, consistently labeled magical and exotic items from every corner of Speria. If all of this was in Klu's private collection, Raz paled to think what might be contained in the Master's vaults sealed deep below the monastery.

But where does one start when pilfering through a Kung Fulio master's secret stash? All that time searching and it felt like they'd only scratched the surface of what Klu's impossibly vast collection had to offer.

"Where do you have to go to find stuff like this…?" Raz wondered aloud.

"Beats me! All I know is, this stuff is

AMAAAAAAZING," Rin said gleefully, rifling through a collection of enchanted broaches with one hand and picking up a golden urn with the other.

"Yeah, but how do we actually, you know, USE any of it? Klu didn't bother to leave instructions."

Rin shrugged, unconcerned, and resumed his search. Raz looked around for a gap in the shelves and started to walk through it.

"Where you going? We're only on shelf number ten of ninety six!" Rin pleaded, with his big eyes wide with concern.

"All these shelves are giving me a headache," Raz sighed. "I'm gonna try the front of the room again."

After a minute or so of aimless wandering, Raz found himself confronted by a bookshelf, two stories tall, shaped

to fit the stone wall's natural curve. The bookshelf was, he
knew, at the back of the room.

The place was so dense he'd somehow managed to
get turned around. It wasn't even the first time. If the
roundabout logic of the Moonken Masters was a place -
this would be it - a dense maze of stuff leading to nowhere.
Even the room was an unnecessary contradiction: half of it
dominated with shelves, half of it nearly wide open.

Grumbling, he resigned to take the long way back to
the front by following the curve of the huge bookshelf. With
a wave of relief, he breached the semi-circle maze of shelves
and arrived back at the front of the room where there was a
relaxing lack of choice.

Magical golden-red light radiated from the leaves
above.

On the far wall to the left was a traditional weapons rack,
chock full of lethal blades. To the right were several wooden
pedestals holding rune-covered books that hovered inches
above the surface. They hung open as if waiting to give
readers a glimpse of some tantalizing forbidden knowledge.

Several wooden dummies were arranged nearby, each
decked out with armor and enchanted objects of some kind.
One, in particular, caught Raz's eye. On its shoulder was
a large folded cloth with small silver bells attached at the
edges with leather hoops. Raz absentmindedly flicked at one
of the bells. A small clear ring reverberated throughout the
chamber.

He read the paper tag but didn't recognize the symbols.
*Come on, Master Klu, give me some sort of hint here. Anything a
couple of desperate trainees could use to scare off a gang of ruthless
thugs?*

Hanging on the wall was a line of glowing scrolls
displaying moving pictures of Moonken warriors. He stood
transfixed for several moments then almost without realizing
it began to move in timing with the scroll. At the end of the

sequence, three glowing words appeared.

"Kwoh...Kai...Tak?" he muttered with uncertainty. Much to his surprise, he felt a pulse of hot energy travel through his body and extend to his fingertips.

Turning, he scanned the shelves to find Rin. Though he couldn't see him, he could hear him rummaging around like a rat in a kitchen.

"Hey Rin!" he called out in the general direction of the shelves, at a volume that was still somewhat discreet. "You know those rune... thingies in the old alphabet that Dou's always droning on about?"

"You mean the ancient Moonken runic script?" Rin clarified as if knowing this were the most normal thing in the world.

"Yeah, whatever. How do you pronounce the one..." he waited for it to appear on the scroll, "the one that looks like two sideways triangles with the three dots over it?"

There was a pause as Rin translated Raz's colorful interpretation into actual information. "Taan," he finally shouted back.

Armed with new information, Raz carefully reproducing the movements shown on the scroll again.

Okay. Here goes nothing.

"Kwoh Kai...TAAN!"

The letters on the scroll glowed then there was a flash of light. Two flames abruptly burst forth from Raz's palms. Then, the skin of his hands turned into black, volcanic rock.

"Oh crap!" Raz yelped in panic. Now he'd done it. He'd lit himself on fire.

"Riiiiin...?" Raz squeaked cautiously, very slowly rotating toward the back of the room. "RIIIIIIIIN! You MIGHT want to have a look at this..." he said more forcefully.

Rin emerged with a clunk, carrying a pile of objects twice his height, which he dropped the instant he saw Raz.

He ran up and studied Raz intently, his eyes glittering like a prospector facing down a big gold strike.

"Whoooooa...good work! You lit yourself on fire!" he exclaimed as if this were a good thing. "How do you stop it?"

"I... don't... know..."

Throwing caution to the wind, Rin hesitantly poked a finger into the flame. He let out a sharp cry of pain and withdrew it.

"Why'd you do that?!" Raz demanded.

"I don't know! I've never tried to stop someone from catching fire!?" Rin shook out his finger and sucked on it. "Owwwww... Not gonna lie, I'm not exactly sure why I expected anything different. It doesn't hurt you?"

Amazingly, it did not. Raz felt no pain, and shook his head as he stared at his hands in wonderment. He was starting to get weirdly comfortable with the stoney-fire hands situation.

"Hold on... I've got an idea," Raz muttered. He extended his palm and flexed his fingers as if to give the flame a little push.

A fireball shot off his hand and hit a small, floral-patterned cushion, which instantly ignited. The two boys gasped in unison and stamped on it to smother the flame. Rin caught his breath as Raz looked down at his hands. With his concentration broken, the remaining flame died out and the skin returned to normal.

Rin and Raz's eyes met, then they both looked back at the scrolls on the wall. With a gentle shove, Rin moved Raz aside.

"Exkewwwwwwwwwze me!" he said and jogged over to the scrolls, rolling them up one by one and throwing them into his bag. "I think these'll do just fine," he exclaimed.

"Damn right, they will," Raz agreed. He'd just summoned magic fire from his hands, and it was awesome. "Why the heck didn't the masters teach us THIS kind of stuff?"

"Alright, Rin," he said, "I think we've got enough to make those Cobra buttheads think twice before they mess with us again. Now let's get out of here. It must be close to sunrise by now. It's a miracle the old man hasn't noticed us down here already!" Raz reasoned. Besides, he couldn't shake the feeling that they weren't alone.

"You're right! Mission accomplished! Just gimme a sec to figure out how I'm going to carry all of this stuff." Then he ran off to begin gathering anything he could fit in his robes.

Raz looked down again at the singed cushion at his feet. Without a doubt, the tacky pillow was Klu's. It was clear he spent a great deal of time in this place.

In front of Klu's smoldering cushion, was a small handmade wooden shelf. He took a few steps closer and saw a statue of a Twilight Monk, Torra maybe, with several pieces of incense burning near it. It reminded Raz of a memorial shrine.

Sitting in front of the statue were three clay figures of horrific bestial demons with humanoid features.

On the right was a four-winged bird, who gripped two gnarled battle axes in its jagged claws. The leftmost statue was a massive bear, bone-like spikes jutting out of its spine and at every joint. In one hand were a set of razor-sharp claws; in the other, it held a giant warhammer caked in dirt and grime.   Finally, in the middle was a toad-like creature, covered in tough scales, wearing a cloak and carrying a spear at least twice as long as its body. The slitted eyes were full of seething hatred. Raz shuddered. It was like the eyes were staring right at him.

Hesitating, he picked up the toad demon statue and turned it over in his hands. It was alarmingly lifelike, each minute detail meticulously recreated. There was no tag, no label. Nothing. He turned the statue over and saw a word scratched on the base in Klu's messy handwriting:

Doken.

Raz scrunched up his face in confusion. What the flyin' heck is a Doken? Raz picked up the bird and saw a different word scratched onto its base.

As he contemplated the demonic shapes, Raz suddenly sensed a presence right behind him. He jumped in surprise, sending the statue of Doken clattering to the floor.

"Mission assets for Operation Cobra Fall are ready for extraction," Rin reported enthusiastically. Despite the pile of objects he had stuffed into his robes and piling up over his arms, he hadn't heard him coming.

"Dude. We need to have a talk about your annoying habit of sneaking up on people out of nowhere," Raz grumbled.

"More like you need to hone your senses to detect my sweet ninja skills," Rin replied, his voice muffled by the mountain of stuff his face was buried in. Rin rotated his entire body so he could see clearly. "Whatcha lookin' at?"

Raz frowned and found the terrifying eyes of Doken looking up at him from the floor. "Not sure exactly," he replied. "Looks like some sort of weird demon statue or something. They're not labeled like the other stuff."

Rin squatted and carefully balanced his load to take

a closer look at the small figurine. "Whoa, they're SUPER detailed," he observed. "You think Klu made 'em?"

"Were you there when he showed us his, uh, 'self-portraits' last week? I'd say Klu's style is a little more... impressionistic," Raz recalled.

"Good point," Rin conceded. He nodded his head towards the shelf of statues, "Think we should take one with us?" he wondered, shifting his weight to keep the pile from toppling in his hands. Raz shook his head immediately.

"No," he said quickly then clarified, "I mean, I don't think they do anything. Besides, they give me the creeps."

"If you say so," Rin replied as he rose to his feet. The strain of lifting the pile made it shift, and a small shiny object toppled from the top as Rin's eyes went wide in panic.

"Raz! Catch it!" Rin ordered.

Raz shot out his right hand to intercept the falling item and immediately felt a literal stab of pain as a long, threading needle stuck into his palm.

"OW! Dammit! What the heck, Rin? WHY WOULD YOU TELL ME TO CATCH A NEEDLE?!" Raz cried out, pulling out the metal object and tossing it on the ground in anger.

"Oops! Well I didn't know what it was!" Rin explained, eyes shifting from side to side guiltily. "But uh...good job? I mean, technically, you did catch it."

Raz groaned and shook out his hand. A small bubble of blood pooled on the surface.

"Ugh, whatever. Why would we need a measly threading needle to defeat the Cobras anyway?" Raz questioned.

Rin coughed awkwardly.

"Well, the tag said it was a, uh, self-threading needle, and I do a lot of sewing so..." Rin stopped as Raz held up a single finger.

"Keep your mind on the mission, man! We're just

here for something to deal with Nox! Remember?" Raz wondered, circling around Rin to maintain eye contact as the big Moonken tried to turn and hide behind his ill-gotten booty.

"Y-Yeah...duh. It's not like I would take it to work on some...uh..." Rin paused to let out what was a mixture of a cough and a laugh, both unconvincing, "some sort of... amazing... secret... team... ninja outfit. That would be ridiculous, and you should feel ashamed for even suggesting it."

Raz stared at Rin blankly for several seconds then shook his head. "Whatever, man. As long as we've got what we need to take on the Cobras. Let's get out of here already," Raz grunted and bent over to pick up the statue of Doken.

The minute the statue made contact with the blood on his palm, it began to change. It was subtle at first. The dull, dust-covered clay shifted slightly in color, becoming brighter - it's lifelike features, even more visible. Then, the cold stone grew hotter, so hot that Raz yelped and tried to let go but it stayed stuck to his palm. It began to burn.

"AUGH! GET OFFA ME DEMON TOAD!" Raz screamed and pried the statue loose. The figurine skittered to the floor, then started to clatter and shake as if some inner force was moving it. Raz stared in disbelief as a final drop of blood levitated from the pinprick on his palm to the statue, where it absorbed into it. The statue pulsed with a dull red light, and smoke rose from it like a fire had been ignited from within its stone shell. Panicked, Rin rapidly shuffled backward, and ran straight into a large brass gong.

GOOOOYOOYONG!

The sound echoed loudly throughout the space. Rin's entire pile of assorted objects fell in a scattered heap to the floor. No way Klu didn't hear that.

The statue continued to writhe around like a wounded animal. As it twirled, the golden-red light from the leaves

above began to shift into a sickly purple-blue as if reacting to a new presence in the room.

"Raz, what did you do?!" Rin said, frantically pushing himself backward as far away as he could to get from danger.

"Remember how I said that statue looked really detailed?"

"Yeeeah…?"

"Let's just say I don't think that's because of Klu's artistic ability."

Raz planted his feet, ready for whatever was coming next.   Rin's eyes widened in horrified realization.

As if in response, the statue's movements changed. It swirled like a top in reverse, slowly bringing itself upright. A thick column of purple-black smoke oozed from the cracks in its surface.

The statue had increased in size from six inches to just under four feet tall. The sinister eyes that had transfixed Raz before suddenly moved in their stone sockets and glowed a fiery yellow from under enormous, scaly lids - fixated directly on the two, puny, unarmed Moonken before him.

All at once, the stone of the statue shattered. Raz and Rin shielded their eyes as the thick, noxious smoke billowed outwards, stinging their throat and eyes. From the column of smoke, they could hear a voice in a horrible language that felt like the squealing crack of ice when exposed to heat.

The smoke cleared and they saw a muscle-bound, larger version of the statue - fully formed. It's thick body and arms covered with armor-like scales the color of rotten wood. Wispy black hair hung down the back of its wide head and drifted over chains and wooden trinkets hung around its neck and ears. It swung a huge spear above its head, no longer stone but real and razor-sharp, sending chunks of encasing stone clattering to the floor as it did.

It opened its huge jaw and let out a loud, croaking roar

that echoed off the stone walls.

   The demon toad Doken had returned to life - and it was pissed.

CHAPTER 6
DOKEN THE TOAD DEMON

Earlier that day, Raz had worried Nox might see him and give him a wedgie he wouldn't forget. Now, face to face with a reawakened demon, far below the ground where no one could hear you scream, his earlier worries felt a tad bit silly. Doken, the demon toad swirled the spear in front of him in a terrifying display of deadly martial skill.

He could have run. But he knew that deep down if it weren't for him, Doken would still be nothing but a supremely disturbing paperweight. No, this was his mess - Rin's too. He raised his hands in front of him, ready to fight.

"Raz, what are you doing?! I don't think we're qualified for this!" Rin shouted. That much was true. Raz watched Doken's eyes flash around the room, taking stock of its surroundings.

"If you wanna ask our toad friend to let us go, be my guest," Raz said. "Otherwise, I think we're the only ones around to stop him."

"Stop... HIM?!" Rin squeaked.

The blood in Raz's veins turned to ice as Doken crouched down like a loaded spring. Then he lunged forward, the massive spear pointed directly towards Rin. Without thinking, Raz shoved his partner aside to safety and found the jagged steel rushing at him instead.

Forcing his stiff legs to obey, he dropped into a squat. In a moment of surreal clarity, Raz watched a tuft of his own severed white hair float in front of his face.

Doken croaked in surprise when his blade struck wood instead of flesh. Before the toad could recover, Raz rolled to his left, putting space between himself and Rin.

"Rin! Better figure out how to use all that junk! And

FAST!" Raz shouted.

Rin leapt over to the remnants of his pile, rummaging through it as fast as he could.

A guttural croak erupted from the demon's mouth. He twirled the spear around himself with a high level of martial skill.

"That's one tough toad!" Raz muttered then jumped straight backward, narrowly dodging several highly-controlled stabs.

"Oof!" he gasped as his back rammed into one of the curved shelves. Desperate for something to defend himself, he grasped blindly behind him and pulled out the purple bag of Size Dust.

Doken's spear flashed again. With nowhere to run, Raz scattered the Size Dust in front of him and hoped for the best. The cloud of purple powder shrank and adhered to the spear as it edged closer. Moments before the razor-sharp point pierced Raz's chest, the weapon shrank to the size of a letter opener, bouncing off of him like a toothpick.

"HOLY CRAP! Way to go, Raz!" Rin cheered excitedly from over the demon's shoulder.

"HAH!" Raz laughed, heart racing, "I TOTALLY knew that would happen!"

Not wasting time, Raz retaliated with a jumping kick. The demon toad reacted with little more than a twitch, shaking off the blow like a horse swatting a fly with its tail. Raising his hand, Doken struck the Moonken with a savage backhand.

"Owwww... well, I at least I got rid of that spear," Raz groaned, rubbing the back of his head.

"Damn right! You're a regular friggin' demon hunter! Now, time for the big guns!" Rin shouted and shoved the moving fire scroll into Raz's hands. "Quick! Do the fireball thing while he's disarmed!"

"Y-Yeah, sure. No problem," Raz replied as if to

convince himself. "One deep-fried toad, comin' right up!"

Frantically, he tried to perform the movements from memory, occasionally glancing at the scroll. It was harder when the pressure was on, and he kept screwing up, having to restart.

Doken croaked a few words in a forgotten ancient tongue and passed his hand over the miniaturized spear. It returned to full size, expelling the purple Size Dust back into the air in a small poof.

"What? This demon knows how to use this stuff more than we do!" Rin squealed, then removed a stack of maps from a large barrel and leaped inside for cover.

"BAH! Come on, you stupid scroll!" Raz swore to himself, trying to focus on the movements. In a fit of rage, Doken wheeled towards Raz, swiping the spear across the shelf, shattering dozens of priceless artifacts.

Rin poked his head out of the barrel, "Quicker, Raz! Quicker! He's coming this way!"

The demon charged, raking the blade of his spear across the ground, kicking up a shower of sparks. Raz tried his best to ignore the certain death bearing down on him. With a shaky voice, he said the glowing words on the scroll, ready to unleash fiery armageddon.

"K-Kwoh Kai Taak!" he shouted, raising his palms out in front of him. A spark of energy surged from his chest, through his forearms and into his fingertips and then…

…*Poof.*

A harmless puff of black smoke burped from his palms. Rin yelped and ducked his head into the barrel like a turtle.

The spear raced towards him again in a downward slice. Raz threw the scroll out in front of him and jumped backward. The blade carved through the scroll-like butter, cleaving it in two - the glowing words faded into plain ink, their power lost in an instant.

Doken's webbed foot pounded into Raz's chest, sending

him flying through the air towards Rin's hiding spot. Rin popped up out of the barrel, spreading his arms wide to catch his friend. "Don't worry buddy, I got y-OOF!"

Raz and Rin crashed together in a tangle of limbs as they tumbled onto the floor. Doken croaked and scanned the room again. Fixing his eyes on the still-open entrance, the demon toad started to walk away from them.

"Raz! He's distracted! Remember Shadowmaster Kito? Time for a tactical retreat!"

"Screw that! We can't let that toad out of here!" Raz said, shaking the glass and splinters of wood from his hair.

"But..."

"No one's gonna thank us for dealing with Nox if we unleash a demon toad on the island!" Raz glanced down at the assorted magical objects on the floor. "Rin, I need you to find the best, most badass, craziest thing you've got, and I need you to do it in the next fifteen seconds!"

Rin swallowed and looked at Raz with a mixture of fear and awe. He nodded affirmingly.

" Okay. But how will I—?"

"Don't care! Just do it and follow my lead!" Raz shouted, and started running in the exact opposite direction his instincts told him to go - towards the demon. He slid to a stop between the entrance and the demon, his arms spread wide.

"Not so fast, big boy!" he shouted, inwardly cursing

himself for saying something so lame at a crucial moment.
Doken tilted his head to the side in curiosity and amusement.
Raz felt lightheaded, like he was occupying someone else's
body and simply watching the spectacle play out from
somewhere warm and safe, far away.

"What? You think I'm done with you, Doken?" Raz
shouted. The demon recoiled at the sound of his name. Raz's
eyes twitched sideways at Rin, who was rifling relentlessly
through the pile.

The demon growled and uttered a string of angry words
in the horrible tongue, pointing back towards the shelf of
other statues then at the entrance. Raz got the sense that it
had a bone to pick with someone topside. Meanwhile, Rin
was moving closer with something in his hand.

That's it...just a little bit longer, Raz thought as a bead of
sweat ran down his forehead. The demon took a deep breath
and blew a puff of noxious purple smoke from its nostrils.

Doken twirled the spear back into its ready hands
and prepared to charge. Simultaneously, Rin was raising
something above his head.

"NOW!" Raz screamed.

With a shrill battle cry, Rin jumped into the air and
threw a long golden urn at the back of Doken's head. It
smashed against the demon's thick scales, releasing a cloud of
purple and red smoke. The smoke escaped the shattered urn,
swirling around the demon as if it were alive with glittering
lights. The plume started to twist and expand, forming into
the shape of a large purple dragon that barely squeezed into
the crowded walls and pressed against the ceiling of the
room.

"Now, that's what I'm talking about!" Raz roared with
excitement.

The toad sneered, twirled the spear around his body
and crouched into a defensive stance, one webbed hand

extended in front of itself. The smoke dragon grew larger
yet. As it spread out its large claws toward the ceiling,
the light from the leaves changed yet again into an almost
exuberant purple and gold. Purple horns shimmered on the
dragons head like they were made of glistening gemstones.

Doken looked nervous.

A clatter of drums, summoned from the spiritual
void itself, sounded against the walls. A voice, terrible and
powerful, then filled the room.

"BEHOLD, MERE MORTALS! YOU SIT IN THE
PRESENCE OF THE WISE AND POWERFUL UMU!"
the dragon bellowed. Umu, the ethereal dragon, bent down
and fixed its glowing eyes on Doken.

"THE GREAT UMU CAN SEE CLEARLY INTO
THE WEBS OF DESTINY, UNDERSTANDING THE
MOST CHALLENGING OF MYSTERIES WITH

Umu

EASE. SUCH IS UMU'S MIGHTY INTELLECT AND INCREDIBLE POWER," said the ethereal form of Umu with great magnificence.

Doken snarled and tightened his grip around the spear, yelling a challenge towards the dragon.

"HA! UMU'S GENIUS IS UNBOTHERED BY SUCH CRASS VULGARITY, FOR HIS WISDOM EXTENDS BEYOND TIME AND SPACE. COME! UMU IS CAPABLE OF TELLING THE FORTUNES OF ANY BEING, EVEN A CREATURE AS COARSE AND LACKING IN PULCRITUDE AS YOU!"

"Did he say...telling fortunes?" Raz gulped.

The remark hadn't gone unnoticed by Doken, either. The toad reared back and drew air into his lungs, inflating his body until it was several times its normal size. All at once, he blew out a massive gust, dissipating the form of the great and powerful Umu with a pathetic poof.

The golden light of the leaves faded into a sickly purple once more, and everyone in the room sat for moments in stunned silence.

Rin swore loudly and began ransacking the pile again for something else he could throw at the creature.

"Well, that was... unhelpful!" Raz observed.

"How was I supposed to know it was just gonna summon a worthless know-it-all?!" Rin replied.

Doken let out a growling hiss that Raz assumed was a laugh, then turned towards the exit, unbothered by the pitiful creatures standing in its way.

Desperate to stop him, Raz ran into the toad's eye line again.

"Hey, where do you think you're going, toad-face? We aren't done with you yet!" he shouted.

At the sound of his name, Doken stopped and glared at Raz in silence. "Ooooh, don't like it when I use your name, huh? Don't blame ya, with a name that stupid I'd be angry too."

"Uhhh Raz... Are you sure you want to piss him off even more than he already is?" Rin called out.

As long as it keeps him down here, Raz thought, staring into the demon's eyes defiantly.

Doken levered his jaw open like a clamshell to an unnatural size and strode forward.

"What? No comeback?" Raz taunted. "Got something you wanna say to me you ugly piece of—"

The thick wet mass of the creature's tongue shot out, latching onto the center of Raz's forehead before he could finish his thought. Frantically, he clawed at the slimy mucus-covered muscle attached to his face, half blind save for one eye that remained uncovered.

"Eeeeewwww! Gross! Let go of him Raz!" Rin advised.

"Ack! I can't! He's got my face, man! Why the face?!" Raz screamed in a nasally whine, his nose now enveloped by the mass of pink flesh. It felt a lot like being smothered by a wet towel covered in snot.

The demon lifted Raz straight into the air, then slammed him down through the weapons rack and into the stone floor, driving the air from his lungs. Raz gasped and squirmed as Doken's tongue picked him up and slammed him down repeatedly.

"Hey, ugly! Let go of my friend!" Rin shouted, circling Doken and scoring little shin kicks that did as much damage to the toad as a mouse nibbling at a dragon. After deftly dodging a few of Doken's angry kicks, Rin circled wider, his hands full of various magical objects. Raz frantically punched and kicked at the tongue.

"Get him offa me!" Raz shouted as Doken's tongue retracted and drew him closer.

"I'm trying! I'm still workin' out how to use all this stuff!" Rin said, dodging Doken's spear stabs with surprising agility.

"JUST CHUCK 'EM!" Raz ordered.

Rin grabbed a crystal with four sharp points and threw it. It hung in the air, radiating a rainbow of colors and shattered before making impact. Next was a golden orb. It scored a direct hit and exploded on Doken's cheek in a poof of green sparks. He threw object after object, and while some of their effects were surprising or strange, they did nothing to damage the demon.

Raz felt the grip of the creatures tongue tighten on his forehead.

"Owww owww owww! I think you're just making him angrier! Whatever you were saving for Nox, use it now!" Raz screamed, but the sound of Rin's attack had died away. Raz pried open one eye to get a better look.

Rin's hands were empty. He'd used, or at least tried to use, every object he'd carefully curated for the purpose of kicking Nox's ass. All shattered or sliced apart with no effect.

"S-Stay back!" Rin cried and pulled out one of his homemade ninja stars as a last resort. The demon toad, still holding Raz with his tongue, raised his spear toward Rin, who froze like a startled deer.

As Doken's rage grew against Rin, Raz felt the grip of the tongue weaken. Using the unexpected slack, he resisted the pull of the tongue enough to grab for something - anything. He felt his hands close around a splinter of broken wood. Doken raised the spear toward Rin.

Now or never, Tenza!

He swung the piece of wood with all the power he could muster - power he didn't even know he had. It thudded into the tongue and sent out a disgusting spray of blood. Doken roared in pain, which was enough to jerk Rin back to his senses. He jumped back out of range.

With a jolt, Raz was reeled in until he was eye to eye with the demon toad. As a Moonken, Raz had seen many looks of hatred and anger in his time, but this topped them all. There were lethal urges in its gaze, ones not born of fear or misunderstanding, but pure murderous rage.

Raz kicked and punched at the toad's body and legs. It groaned, more a sound of mild annoyance than pain.

Doken drew in a huge breath, inflating his body once more and opening his jaws wide. Raz felt his legs being lifted off the ground. The tongue was reeling in to the mouth, leaving Raz overcome with the stench of rotten fish and sulfur.

I hope he's not doing what I think he's doing!

Like a fisherman making one final pull at the line, Doken tilted his head back and went to swallow Raz whole. The lips of the toad's gaping jaw engulfed him. Then, darkness.

Lucky for Raz, as big as Doken was, he wasn't quite large enough to fit the entire body of the teenage Moonken in his belly whole. Raz's descent into the demon's gut stopped abruptly, leaving his legs from the knee down dangling precariously in the air out of Doken's gullet. The toad's eyes went wide with surprise as he tipped backward unexpectedly, falling heavily onto the stone floor.

From within the blackness of the toad's vile stomach, Raz felt Doken fall onto his back. He kicked and thrashed furiously until his legs were halfway free, and rolled leveraging his weight to get onto his feet.

Here goes nothing!

Completely blinded, with his head stuck in the demon toads mouth, Raz stood up. Doken's body twitched in the air as if Raz were wearing the toad like a horrific oversized hat.

Unable to determine who now had the upper hand, Rin squealed as he wailed on Doken with what Raz could only assume was a piece of shelving. The strikes sent thudding reverberations through the demon's stomach. The mixture of surprise and pain made Doken's grip slip a little more.

It was enough.

With the jaw around his upper body loosened, Raz battered, punched and bit the inside of the toad's throat. What the blows lacked in precision they made up for in ferocity. Doken twitched and writhed in discomfort.

With a retching croak, Raz was launched free, covered in a thick layer of mucus and slime.

"Raz! You're alive!" Rin called out and ran over to him as if to embrace him but stopped short, his nose wrinkling. "Though you couldn't tell by the smell."

"Oh, You think it SMELLS bad? Try livin' in it for a few minutes!" Raz replied, elated to be undigested.

The toad hacked and spat thick streams of green slime onto the stone floors, and groped for his spear. He bent his legs into a deep crouch and launched himself upwards, high over the two Moonken. On the way down, he kicked the shelf behind them, causing it to wobble and fall on top of them.

"DUCK!" Rin called out. The shelf crashed to the ground, propped up only by the other scattered objects on the floor. But they were in bad shape - they were pinned. Raz looked up towards the ceiling, up towards Klu's dojo. Hadn't the old man heard ANY of this?

They felt Doken land on the top side of the shelf. Soon after, the spear point rocketed through the wood between their faces. They tried to roll to avoid the onslaught. Doken rammed his spear into the shelf again in blind rage, hoping to hit flesh.

Then the stabbing stopped as a jovial and familiar laugh echoed within the chamber.

"Hooooh ho ho, hee hee!"

Blue smoke flooded the entire cavern from wall too wall along the surface of the floor. There was a thud from the center of the room. Raz could faintly make out a blurry humanoid figure. Doken immediately took notice. The demon's muscles stiffened and it carefully crouched into a disciplined fighting stance. It was not playing anymore. *Oh crap, did we wake another one up?*! Raz thought, looking for somewhere to hide.

The mystery figure threw their arms out to the side and spun around the room like a top, coming to a stop in front of Raz and Rin. The force of the movement parted the smoke and Raz saw that this was no demon, but a Moonken. Several large coy fish tattoos wrapped themselves around the man's wiry and muscular back.

The mysterious warrior flexed his exposed muscles. He wore orange shorts with no shoes, each toe spread out wide as if to strengthen their connection with the earth. Long, heavy ears were neatly concealed by a bulk of white dreadlocks weighed down with heavy metal beads.

The elder Moonken's arms effortlessly flowed in a continuous circle, and the smoke in the room gathered around him. He planted his feet firmly into the earth and the smoke blew away. Doken made no move to attack, it only watched and observed.   The warrior's hands curled at the wrists into a style Raz recognized as the Mantis form of the fighting style known on the island as Kung Fulio. The impressive figure, reminded Raz of the statues outside. A savior literally had dropped in from above to destroy evil, summoned by the darkness.

It looked to him, to carry the same presence as that of the ancients, the Monks of Twilight.

The mysterious Moonken grunted and scratched at his short goatee, then turned and grinned back at the two boys. Hanging from the side of his mouth was a long, golden smoking pipe, which he shifted from one side of his mouth to the other. Its filigree pattern work was old, and carved in shapes Raz had not seen anywhere else in Speria. But he'd seen it in the monastery plenty of times. His long white hair bundled together in heavily threaded dreadlocks, which swung over his shoulders whenever he turned.

"M-Master Klu?!" the two boys stammered in unison. With the smoke cleared, an entirely new view of the situation arose.   The shapes of flowing garments turned out to be loose pajamas, covered in stains and holes. Klu shifted his pipe to the other side of his mouth, winked, and turned his attention back to the demon toad.

"Back to your world of shadow and stone, Doken!" Klu bellowed in a voice that echoed throughout the chamber. The assertiveness of his tone didn't feel like Klu at all. Surely there was some kind of mistake. It couldn't be him.

Doken, the furious warrior toad, looked at the old Master and shook with anger, pointing its finger and spitting out insults in its horrible tongue.

"Brah!" Klu gasped in a wounded tone of voice, "No need for that kind of language, man!"

Nope. That was him, alright.

Doken roared a savage cry from deep in its twisted belly and lunged at the old Master. But the old man was quick, shockingly quick. Before Doken was airborne, Klu had already begun to move. He effortlessly stepped out of the way.

As the shaft of the spear passed, Klu struck it with his open palm, deflecting the blade into a nearby shelf. Before Doken could pull it free, Klu stomped down on the handle, causing Doken to surge forward into a waiting fist. Doken flew back, disarmed, rolling head over heels.

The old Moonken yawned. With fluid, almost lazy, yet elegant movement, he broke the spear's blade from the handle with a stiff open-handed chop. He rolled his shoulders forward and back and rubbed his thumb across his large nose. His eyes were dull and unfocused, like he was ready to fall asleep at any moment.

Doken rose, shaking his head in a daze, as Klu swayed like a piece of seaweed at the bottom of the ocean. Doken opened his jaw wide, ready to lash out with the tongue once more.

"Look out!" Raz called out in feeble warning. Klu responded by yawning again, covering his mouth with his hand politely. Even in a battle of life and death, there was no need to rush.

The pink blur of Doken's tongue forcefully launched at Klu's face. The same tongue attack that he'd used earlier on Raz. The old master merely cricked his head to one side, eyes still closed, and the tongue passed harmlessly over his shoulder. At the last moment, he opened his eyes, reached up and gripped the sticky mass of muscle between two pinched fingers.

It twitched and writhed in Klu's powerful grip as Doken frantically tried to pull it back into its mouth. The old Kung Fulio master slowly spun towards Doken. He moved with the grace of a dancer, every step like the rehearsed steps of a waltz. As he moved, he wove his arms in complicated circles, tightly coiling Doken's tongue around his left arm like a rope. The old man surged forward, until he was standing nose to nose with the beast.

The blow from the toad's tightly coiled fist came hard and fast. Rin and Raz gasped.

Though the strike seemed to hit, Klu melted away from it harmlessly. With the toad's tongue still solidly trapped, Klu retorted with several kicks to Doken's face. Several more blows lashed out toward Klu, but he flowed around them. For every punch Doken threw, Klu struck Doken twice more.

Doken, deciding enough was enough, jumped up and kicked his captor with both of his sturdy legs. The old man released the tongue right at the point of impact, causing Doken merely to launch himself backward. The tongue snapped violently back into Doken's mouth like a taut rubber band.

"Whoa…" Raz stood with his jaw open and stared

in amazement. The idea of getting to safety was quickly supplanted by the incredible show of martial arts mastery before them. At any rate, Doken didn't care about them or even about escaping anymore - it wanted Klu's head.

With a savage kick, Doken bounced off a shelf. It toppled backward, causing a domino effect with the shelves behind it, which echoed into the sound of shattering glass and clanging metal.

The demon flew at Klu from the air, and the old master effortlessly, almost lazily weaved away. He twisted this way and that, as Doken furiously flew past him again and again from every conceivable angle. With another yawn, Klu tipped backward, forming a bridge. It was a familiar move. Not but a week earlier, Klu had gotten all the students to hold this position as they looked out at the seascape upside down. In fact, Raz recognized many of the poses that Klu now used to fight. But seeing them in action was something else. He began to wonder if Klu knew more moves than he realized. At the time, it didn't seem like there could be much martial use in moves like that. But now he saw that he'd been wrong.

As Doken passed overhead, Klu rolled up and shot both legs upward into his opponent's stomach, sending him straight up into the air, then crashing down to the stone floor - hard. Doken climbed to his feet, shook his head, jumped up, faked a left hook, and then came at Klu hard with his clenched right fist.

Raz winced as if the blow were meant for him, but unlike him, Klu didn't fall for the feint. He held Doken's fist with one hand and gently moved it aside, bringing their faces within inches of one another.

With his free hand, he took the pipe out of his mouth and blew a plume of blue smoke into the creature's face. The toad stumbled backward, rubbing its eyes, and cursing in the same infernal tongue. He swiped blindly at the air in front of him.

Klu blinked a few times, then swept Doken's legs out from under him. He then extended two fingers into the air and brought them down on Doken's neck. The demon twitched furiously, but did not thrash or kick. Somehow, Klu had subdued it. The old master cleared his throat.

"Alright mah dude, you had your fun," he said and turned to his two stupefied students. "Yo, brah, could one of you, like, grab that Sash of Containment up at the front?"

"Sash of what now…?" Raz croaked, not taking his eyes off of the demon.

"Ahhhh, right! Like, how are you gonna know that?!" Klu chuckled, in a surprisingly casual demeanor. "The cloth thingy with the little silver bells."

"Uhhh…" Raz stammered, trying to remember. It did seem familiar.

"Like, no rush or anything, my little brother, but this hold only lasts for like... so long, you know?"

Raz shook himself to his senses and ran back to the row of wooden dummies. He plucked the strange fabric from it then ran back to the old Master. The hand Klu used to contain the demon was starting to shake, but his face betrayed no signs of panic.

"Cool, cool. Just like... throw that sucker over Doken's head, would ya?" he requested in a lazy drawl.

Raz looked at Doken and gulped. He slowly took a few steps forward, unfurled the cloth and threw it over the demon. The last he saw of Doken was the red, rage-filled eyes.

"Right on, right on!" Klu said enthusiastically, giving Raz the thumbs up with his free hand. "Alright, little dudes, if you could take, like, two, maybe three steps back."

The boys did as they were told and waited patiently for whatever dramatic magical explosion was sure to happen next. Instead, a half-naked Klu jumped back a step, withdrew his flute from who knows where, and began to play a tune. He even shuffled a little jig along with the rhythm.

The sounds of the flute filled the air, and the bells on the sash rang in harmony. The cloth began to tighten and fold on its own as Doken twisted and roared beneath it.

As he played on, the shape under the fabric gradually shrank and then stopped moving. The last note of the flute died off, and Klu gave the two young Moonken a wry smile.

Klu strode forward and tied the cloth up, throwing an object into the air. The old master caught it, studied it and shook his head before tossing it over to Raz, who fumbled it a few times before catching it. In his hands was the toad statue once more, without a spear, and looking angrier than ever.

"What was that...?" Raz asked.

"Oh, that's Doken, an angry and mean little guy," Klu said. "As for what he is, well..." he paused and took a deep drag from his pipe. "That, my little bros, is a Darksprite."

CHAPTER 7
GUNGA LAGUNGA

Various magical trinkets and sacred scrolls lay scattered, broken or torn across the floor of the underground chamber that was Master Klu's secret stash. There was no other way to put it. The entire room had been completely and utterly destroyed.

Master Klu surveyed the entirety of the damage casually, then looked down at his feet and yelped in alarm.

"Awwwww man! My favorite cushion!" The old master sighed mournfully then shuffled pigeon-toed to the remains of the weapons rack. It was hard for Raz to believe that this shambling old master was the same guy that had just wiped the floor with the Demon Toad Doken only moments before. If he hadn't seen it with his own eyes, Raz would hardly believe it happened at all.

Klu stooped down, carelessly tossing aside ancient weapons

like a child rummaging through a toy chest. Finally, he raised a long wooden surfboard in front of him lovingly and let out a long sigh of relief.

"Whoo! That was a close one, wasn't it, Gidgey?" Klu held the board out in front of him, examining it for damage. "Don't worry, papa's gon' take you out again real soon!" He licked his thumb and wiped off a small smudge before gingerly resting it on the floor.

Unable to formulate any kind of excuse, Rin squeaked like a leaking balloon. Raz, confused as to whether or not the punishment was imminent or not, remained silent.

"Wait…" Klu paused. "You lil' dudes ain't s'posed to even like, know about my hidden stash, man." He plodded over to stand in front of them with lazy, yet suspicious eyes.

Nervously, Raz dusted himself off and took a step forward with a limp that was just now forming as the adrenaline wore off.   "It's uh, well… we were just… um, Master Klu we —"

"Whoa whoa WHOA!" Klu shouted in alarm, and took a step back. He crouched slightly and darted his head from side to side, blinking in disbelief as if he'd just noticed the state of the room for the first time. "Man, my STUFF! It's all busted up!"

Klu had a pained look in his eye of a man who'd accidentally lost a family heirloom out in the woods. Guilt crept up on Raz and seized him. Of all the Masters, Klu was everyone's favorite.

He was the only one that didn't treat Raz like an outsider. And now Raz had completely destroyed his prized stash of ancient treasures. Raz began to finally understand. Master Klu didn't NEED to lock the door on his dojo. His lock, his security, was his trust in all of his students. A trust that Raz had blatantly betrayed. As if sensing the dark clouds forming in his student's mind, Klu smirked, his gaze drifted down as he held out his hand.

"Lemme take that off yer hands, l'il dude."

Confused, Raz realized that he was still holding the statue of Doken. Rin jumped back, as he eyed it warily in case it returned to life unexpectedly once more.

"So, before you were saying... about Doken?" Raz said, handing the statue back to Klu as he sauntered over to the small hand-carved shelf and stood it upright, gingerly placing the other two statues in their original spots.

"Doken? Aww, he ain't so bad. Always did have a problem with creating messes though, y' know? Bit of a temper on that guy, Always was." he mused, and used his pipe to relight the incense.   Rin stood upright, "But... what's a Darksprite doing here? Something happen between you two?"

"Yeah, was he, like, your old arch nemesis or something?" Raz chimed in.

But Klu just held the statue of Doken up to his eye line and examined it as if looking for cracks. "Nemesis? Naw man, it ain't like that, see? Doken's just another lost soul, y' know?"

Rin inched closer, peering at the statues from behind the old master. "Isn't it a bit... dangerous to keep rage-filled demons locked up below the monastery?" he suggested.

The old master laughed. "Heh. Old Doken here ain't got nothin on the many hidden secrets buried just under the surface of this here island." Rin and Raz glanced at each other, wild-eyed with the possibilities of what such a statement could mean.

The old Moonken stood frozen in thought as if the question had short-circuited his brain.

"Still, I can't believe it... we were fighting a DARKSPRITE!" Raz said, with a sparkle in his eye. "The ultimate, most evil and nefarious beings in all of Speria! Us!"

Klu furrowed his brow and tilted his head to the side like a shaggy dog.

"Whoa whoa whoa, slow down little man!" Klu said, extending his palms out towards Raz. "Good? Evil? Them's just words, brah! We're ALL just ridin' the same cosmic wave of the universe!"

Klu patted the statue of Doken on the head and put it gently back into its spot between the other two Darksprites. "There ya go ol' Doken. You just rest there a little longer, old friend."

Klu's foot slipped out from under him, and he frantically flapped his arms to regain his balance. He picked a torn piece of brown paper off of his heel.

"Awww man, my original map of Kaajul! I always wanted to go back there again. Best veggie stew in ALL of Speria." He sighed and let the paper drift back to the floor and trotted off towards the back of the room, climbing over downed shelves as he went.

Raz waited until Klu was out of earshot, then sidled over to Rin and nudged him with his elbow.

"Ow! What was that for?"

Mao whispered, "Did you know the old guy was a bonafide legendary badass the whole time?"

Rin shrugged. "Yeah. So?"

"So?!" Raz's shouted, then quickly lowered his voice again. "So I'm thinking that maybe Klu's stash isn't gonna help us."

"No duh. We just trashed it," Rin stated, his face turning

red with embarrassment. "And we didn't find anything we
could use anyway."

"Exactly," Raz agreed. "That plan was, in retrospect, a
little flawed. But don't you see it? We've got the solution to
our little Nox problem right here!"

"You wanna seal Nox in a statue for eternity?" Rin
asked.

"No! I mean HIM!" Raz explained, pointing at Klu,
who was at that moment giggling while he juggled three
jars of Star Jellies, before neatly arranging them on a well
balanced selfing. Rin raised his eyebrow as Raz hustled to
catch up with the master.

"Hey, Master Klu," Raz called out. The master jumped
in surprise, nearly dropping the jars.

"WHOA! Don't scare me like that, brah! If these guys
get out they could like... tear the fabric of the universe, man,"
Putting the jars down into a neat pile on the floor instead.

Raz quickly started to help stack other items that
had survived the onslaught, though finding the items that
remained intact proved somewhat of a challenge. Guessing
what Klu's piles represented or how they might be arranged
was as difficult as understanding the mind of the master
himself.

"Say, about before, I mean, during that fight..." Raz
ventured, trying to position himself into the old Moonken's
eye line. "That was really something back there. I mean,
you're kind of amazing!"

Klu stood and paused his movement, peering at Raz
over his nose. "Whaaaaaa? Me?" he asked finally, to no one
in particular. Raz stuffed a collection of scrolls under his
arm, and shoved them into the little golden urn they'd fallen
out of.

Very helpful. A model student, one might say. He grinned.

"I mean, those MOVES!" Raz exclaimed and mimed
out a few strikes as Klu watched with vacant eyes. "Whattya

call moves like that anyway?"

Realizing that Raz's interest was piqued, the old master glanced at him out of the corner of his eye. "So you have some... interest in... Kung Fulio?"

"Ohhhh, yeah! Big time!" Raz nodded. "Say, how long do you think it'd take for someone to learn some of that Coolio Kung Fulio?" He swung his arms around, poorly imitating the sidestepping move he'd seen the seasoned Master do earlier, until nearly toppling over the last vase in the room.

Klu stared cross-eyed at his fingers as he did a calculation in his head. "I don't know, man, maybe...twenty, thirty..."

"Hours!? Raz interjected excitedly.

"No, no. Years!" the old master replied. "Give or take."

"Interesting, interesting," Raz nodded along complacently.   "But, I mean, there's probably a shortcut or something right?"

"Shortcut?" Klu parroted, kicking around a pouch of Size Dust like a hacky-sack.

"Yeah, like some kind of... legendary, SECRET sort of way?"

"Secret? Hmmmm..." Klu pondered, stroking his goatee.   "You mean like... some kind of *secret* of Kung Fulio?" he asked mysteriously and waggled his fingers for dramatic effect.

"I knew it! There are secret training techniques!" Raz proclaimed, nudging Rin once more with a good I-told-you-so elbow.

In a flash, the ancient master's eyes were half-closed and as vacant as ever. Klu, the wandering warrior, was gone, and Klu the clueless finger-painter, was back. He snickered to himself, snatched a book off the floor and shuffled towards the gigantic bookshelf. He could not be more disinterested.

"Naw. Doesn't really work that way lil' chico. The

ancient and mystical art of Kung Fulio comes to us all in its own time. You can kick and splash around all you want, but in the end, there's nothin' to it but to let go. Take a ride, and move with the motion of the cosmic ocean," he said, extending his arm out in front of him and moving it in a wave as if he were starting some kind of groovy dance.

Raz slid on his knees to stop in front of Klu in a desperate pleading gesture. He bowed his head low in reverence and clasped his hands in front of him. Begging wasn't usually in Raz's rulebook, but if the secrets of martial dominance were within grasp, he was willing to be flexible.

"Master Klu, please! You saw us back there, we went toe to toe with a Darksprite! We're ready to move up to the next level!" Raz begged. Klu ignored him and stepped around him like he was another piece of debris as he began to chant one of his favorite old songs.

Klu smacked his lips a few times as he swapped the positions of a few books on the shelf. "Ready for what now?"

Raz squinted hard, trying to read Master Klu's vacant expression. Despite his personality, Klu was no dummy. The dumb guy act might only be a feint - a clever ruse to throw Raz off the scent.

Or, it was possible Klu's memory had as many holes in it as a moth-eaten shirt.

"Whaddya mean, 'for what'!? To learn the SECRETS OF KUNG FULIO! Obviously!! I'll totally try hard! Harder than you've ever seen! Teach us, o great Master Klu! Teach us the secrets of Kung Fulio!" Raz cried and held his hands out in front of him as if the old master could somehow pull the ability right out of the air and bestow it into his empty hand like an apple.

"Whoa, whoa, whoa, lil chico!" Klu bent his knees and put out his arms like he was riding some immense wave. "Sloooow down! Like I said, everything happens in its own time, man!"

Both Raz and Rin's shoulders sank.

"What's got you dudes worked up enough to seek out my o-so-gnarly stash this evening, anyway?"

In the space of ten seconds, Raz's mind raced back and forth. After everything they'd just seen, he wanted to blurt out the whole problem with Nox. But this was Klu, the master who ran a non-violent dojo and used the weapons to write calligraphy in the sand and bake cookies for late-night munchies.

"Let's just say, if I don't learn how to be the ultimate badass warrior monk in the next twenty-four hours or so, I'm dead," Raz said plainly. He felt a sharp jab of pain as Rin kicked him in the shin.

"Oh, I mean... WE are dead."

"Simmer down, l'il brosephs! A few days ago, you were all like, not even showing up for training, and now you're all fired up?" Klu wondered.

Raz shifted his gaze to the floor. Rin's feet shuffled nervously.

"I... I can't tell you why we need it, but we do," Raz mumbled. "You're probably the only master on this whole island who'd help us. Please."

Klu stopped rearranging the books and turned to study the two defeated faces next to him. "Whoa... Sounds serious!" he said.

"Sounds like you two got yourselves some big problems, brah..." he said quietly. "And big problems... need big solutions. Eh?"

Raz's eyes lit up at. "That's an understatement!".

Klu raised one eyebrow. "No way around it?"

"Nope. No way around it but to fight." Raz replied.

"Welp! If that's the way it's gotta be. Bring it in lil bros." The old master wiggled his fingers in the air. Drawing himself up with a big intake of breath, he stood tall and squinted his eyes as if to rummage through the recesses of his mind, preparing for some sort of ritual. No one dared to move so as not to break the master's concentration. This was it, the moment Raz had been waiting for.

Klu placed a finger on each one of their foreheads rather awkwardly. With his eyes closed, he completely missed Rin's forehead, so the big guy just moved the center of his head to meet wherever the old master's finger pointed. He slowly extended the rest of his fingers one at a time, until each of his hands were spread out over the entirety of the young Moonken's faces. Raz breathed through one squished nostril and squinted his eye. Deep in thought, the old master hummed and grumbled.

This lasted for quite some time - an uncomfortably long time.

Raz felt nothing. He waited and waited, but he felt no different. There was no surge of energy, no exchange of visions or memory, only the musty scent of the old Moonken's palms. Raz cracked his eyes open and saw Master Klu's head lulled to one side; a gentle snore escaped from the back of his throat. Suddenly he snorted, and the old Moonken's eyes popped open as he flung his arms in the air.

"Gunga Lagunga…" Klu whispered.

"Umm, bless you?" Raz offered. Rin coughed in lieu of a response.

"Gunga Lagunga!" Klu shouted the words again and pounded a fist against his tattooed chest. "It's a saying, bruh! Means that whatever happens is like… gonna happen! It's a reminder, yah? Sometimes, ya just need to let it all go! You can't force the waves. Like, when in doubt, ride it out!"

Raising his pipe to his lips, he took a long inhale then continued with a cough, "Like… things tend to work themselves out if you let 'em. But try and force it… well, you think you're movin' forward, but you're just runnin' in circles, y' know?"

"Gunga… Lagunga?" Raz repeated back. "Ride it

out...? Like... just wait for stuff to happen?"

"Yaaah, you got it brah!"

"Gungalag... runga..." Rin fumbled the unfamiliar word on his tongue.

"No, no, no, man! Uuuuun-gah!" Klu sounded it out, pointing at his lips.

"Uuuuun-gaaaah! Gunga Laguguun," Rin tried again. Klu frowned.

"Lagunga."

"Lagoogle."

"Gunga."

Rin closed his eyes and then bellowed out, "Gunga... LAGUNGA!"

Klu actually clapped he was so excited.

Was this some kind of joke? Raz had been in many places and seen many things on his way to Crescent Isle. Strange things. This display reminded him that multiple Moonken in a room was bound to turn weird at some point. And just like always, it pretty much led nowhere.

"Master Klu, that's great and all but—"

Klu's finger smooshed over Raz's mouth clumsily.

"Say no more, li'l man, say no more. Klu gets it. Two of his favorite bros-in-training are in trouble, and they need some help. I know just the thing," he explained.

Klu took off at a fast pace toward the golden scrolls near the half-way point of the room.

"Phew! Good thing these didn't get hit, eh bros? If they did, Dou would like... totally throw a fit," Klu said, shuddering a little. The rack swayed unsteadily as Klu patted it. Raz quietly reached a hand out to stabilize it.

"Yeah, ancient scrolls, priceless knowledge, et cetera, et cetera," Raz said impatiently. "You were saying you had something for us?"

"Huh? Oh, right! Yeah! It'll blow your mind, dude. You need some kind of secret weapon, yah?" Klu asked.

Internally, Raz squealed with delight. That was the problem with their whole plan before: they just didn't know what to look for. Now with Klu to help them, they'd get exactly what they needed. It was the best-case scenario.

Klu flipped a lever and a hidden wall extended another golden rack from the stone wall. A few of the priceless scrolls clattered to the floor. He paid them no mind. The old Moonken stuck out his tongue in concentration as his arm disappeared from view.

A hidden scroll? A devious artifact of some kind? Raz's mouth watered just thinking of the possibilities.

Klu's stopped rummaging. "Here we go, brah!"

Without realizing it, Raz had started quivering with excitement. Next to him, Rin bounced on his toes. Ever so carefully, Klu withdrew his hand and held out a huge cylindrical object wrapped in cloth. Tears formed in the old Moonken's eyes as if he were reunited with an old friend.

"S-Sorry little bruhs. I get… (*sniff sniff…*) emotional and such," he paused and blinked the tears out of his eyes, "I get the feels every time I see it."

Slowly and gently, Master Klu set the object on the floor in front of him where Raz and Rin quickly dropped to their knees out of respect.

"The greatest weapon for the most ambitious of students. A weapon that will unlock the hidden potential sleeping deep inside of you…" Klu began.

He breathed deeply and then unfurled the cloth one corner at a time. Delicately. Raz and Rin craned forward, drawn like a moth to the flame to look at it.

"Master Klu, it's a… it's…" Raz stammered, unsure of what to say.

"It's a carrot!" Klu piped in enthusiastically, confirming Raz's worst fears.

"It sure is…" Rin agreed, reaching out to poke it. The old master slapped his hand away. "Biggest friggin' carrot what you'll ever see!"

"But you said it was the secret to Kung Fulio. A way to unlock my hidden potential," Raz whined.

"Oh… Yah!" Klu confirmed as he admired every inch of it's orange glory. "Most certainly!"

"The secret to Kung Fulio is a balanced diet?" Raz asked.

"Nah man! The carrot IS the secret!" Klu exclaimed and shoved it into Raz's chest, nearly toppling him over.

"Ooof!" Raz gasped.

"Right! I get it… A secret carrot," Rin chimed in like he was following along, though Raz knew he was not.

Raz's face turned white.

A carrot? A lousy, stinking carrot?

In a whirlwind, Klu rose, practically dragging the two bewildered students behind him along the bookcase toward the back of the room. As he walked, he babbled on.

"Like, that's a great carrot. Grew it myself. Left it down here. Forgot it. Spritzed it with some water. Forgot it again… But doesn't matter, man, 'cus it ended up with you!" He glanced back at them and winked. "Right where it was supposed to."

"So is it... a magic carrot?" Raz asked, grunting with exertion under the added weight.

"Magic? Nah brah!"

"Do I... eat it?"

"Whoa! Eat it?!" Klu asked, shocked by the audacity of such a question. "Weren't you LISTENING, bro? Everything you're looking for is in that carrot man. You can't just EAT it!"

"Hold up! Listen, Master. It's not like I'm not... grateful? I guess? But I mean it, Master Klu, we're in SERIOUS trouble! What am I supposed to DO with this?" Raz pleaded.

Klu abruptly halted, his momentum spinning him around on one heel like a weathervane. Suddenly, the entire disposition of the Moonken Master changed. His foot slowly went to the floor and his expression was one of alarming clarity.

"What you do with this carrot will determine the outcome of the rest of your life." Klu said enigmatically, folding his hands behind his back. He strode away with measured and controlled steps. Raz trailed behind.

Klu stopped in front of a bookcase. He rested his finger on a book with a picture of a happy smiling fish on the spine. He pulled the tome from the row and the bookcase swung open, releasing a gust of salty sea air. Klu looked at Raz directly in the eye, as if searching into his soul. Then he gestured to the tunnel behind the bookcase.

"WELP, end of the line, bros! Time to go! Just follow this tunnel and it'll take you right back to the Isle, my dudes. One way ticket."

"Wait, but what about—" Rin stammered but was silenced as Klu firmly placed his hands on his student's backs and shoved them into the tunnel.

"But master I..."

"Gunga Lagunga lil bros! And Raz," Klu called out,

"Take care of that carrot, and it'll take care of you!"

The bookcase slammed shut from the other side, and Raz and Rin found themselves falling in complete darkness. Somehow, impossibly, they burst out the cliffside near the northern gate where they'd started.

Once oriented, Rin inspected the cliffside and found nothing. It was like they appeared out of thin air. Even after his display of Kung Fulio mastery, it seemed Master Klu had a few more tricks up his sleeve yet.

But the whole ordeal left them back where they had started, albeit with a few extra bruises and a carrot the size of a large sack of potatoes. Raz cradled the oversized vegetable and slumped to the ground.

"I can't believe it! All that work for NOTHING?" Raz shouted, kicking dirt over the side of the ledge and into the crashing waves below.

"At least we're not in trouble," Rin said, trying to find the bright side.

"Yeah, I guess. But we're not any closer to beating Nox, either," Raz replied.

"I don't know, maybe Klu's not crazy…" Rin reasoned. They both glanced at the carrot as proof to the contrary. "Okay, he's a LITTLE crazy."

A crack of light appeared on the horizon and Rin shot up like a reed.

"Oh crap! C'mon Raz! Hurry up!" Rin shouted and started scrambling down the rock back to the path.

"What? What's on your mind big guy?" Raz asked, rising to his feet.

"Dou!" Rin exclaimed. Raz raised an eyebrow.

"Uh… I don't think Master Dou's gonna help us, buddy," Raz remarked. "You could start a war on Crescent Isle, and he wouldn't bat an eyelid."

"No, dingus! Master Dou's morning meditation! You didn't forget, did you?"

"What? Master Dou's boring classes? Honestly, don't we have more important things to worry about?" Raz reasoned. "Why don't we skip it today?"

"And let Tomo put us on laundry duty for the rest of the day?" Rin shuddered. "How exactly are we supposed to beat Nox if we end up locked away in the temple scrubbin' the Master's dirty undies?"

Raz scrambled down to the path. "Point taken. But won't Nox be there?"

The two started to jog over to the gate together. "It's like Klu said, don't sweat it! Gunga Lagunga, or whatever! Act natural!"

"Yeah, act natural," Raz mumbled to himself as he slung the mysterious, fifty-pound carrot over his shoulder and ran towards the monastery. He glanced out at the rising sun and heard roosters cry out to signal the start of a new day.

CHAPTER 8
WE'RE GONNA NEED ALLIES

Klu's limp body slammed into the cliff face overlooking the market square, shattering the rock into a thousand splinters. The blow came so fast that even a Master couldn't see it coming. A column of black smoke drifted up from the market as the helpless townspeople screamed and ran for cover. The students of the monastery cowered in the temple - they weren't strong enough to fight such a pure specimen of unfettered evil. The purple dragon, three times the size of Hamcha's BBQ slithered through the air towards Klu, snapping its razor-sharp teeth together in anticipation for its next meal.

Klu reached out his hand feebly, begging for rescue from his certain doom.

Lucky for Klu, Raz Tenza was there - and he could take

on an evil sixty-foot acid-spitting dragon in his sleep.

An ominous voice echoed across the horizon, *"For the Moonken, more than the other creatures in Speria, our way is the way of balance…"*

As soon as the frightened townspeople caught sight of their hero, they cheered ferociously. All of the other students emptied out of the temple to watch. The dragon turned towards Raz, Its fiery red eyes instantly went wide - every creature of evil in Speria lived in fear of the great demon hunter Raz Tenza. The dragon shot out streams of burning acid rapid-fire at Raz, melting the mountain's side to ash. Raz saw it coming a mile away. He weaved and dodged the projectiles without taking a scratch, altering course in mid-air like a living firecracker.

From beyond space and time, that pesky, ominous voice continued, *"We are creatures of extraordinary potential and longevity, capable of great good and great evil alike - thus, we must be mindful of our place in the cosmos. Thus, we are little more than insignificant specks…"*

KA-BOOOOOOOOM!

The force of Raz's kick released an explosion like a crack of thunder. It was the forbidden move, known as the Kick of a Thousand Years of Pain. He followed by punching the dragon seven times, each strike hitting a pressure point that caused the creature to roar in pain. Kicking off the dragon's nose, he landed next to Klu and pulled him out of the cliff face.

"Good thing you showed up, brah."

"Well, someone's gotta watch your butt, old man. Now go! This is MY fight." Raz grumbled as his eyes went white with power. Klu patted him on the back and surfed away down the cliff on his surfboard, which he happened to have with him, obviously.

A few of the students and townspeople, emboldened by Raz's flawless display of Kung Fulio power, came to kick at

the dragon's heels. He landed on the ground between them.
"I can't let you risk yourselves, return to your homes,"
he declared. They stood in awe - the hero, Raz Tenza, in the
flesh.

"Of course, Master Tenza!"

"Go get him, Master Tenza!"

"I wish I could be as strong as you, Master Tenza!"

"Yes, yes, now go, this dragon ain't gonna defeat itself."

*"Thus, the Moonken do not force balance, we live it - we mimic
the indifferent flow of the universe - only by accepting that we are
nothing, that we are no more powerful than an ant, can we unlock our
hidden potential..."*

Raz, the living embodiment of perfect Kung Fulio
power and majesty circled the beast. The dragon shook out
the pain and turned towards him, and ran up the cliff face,
preparing his final blow and...

... and teetered on one leg atop a log, swinging and
flapping his arms wildly for balance as Raz's daydream gave
way to the disappointment of reality.

They had less than twenty-four hours before their
permanent exile, and here he was, balancing on logs as
Master Dou lectured about the celestial bodies or why the
sky was blue or whatever. Another boring class surrounded
by students who hated him while his whole world was at
stake.

*"Perhaps the value of balance, both mental and otherwise, is lost
on the young Raz,"* came Master Dou's booming voice over the
sounds of the roaring river below.

Giggles from the other students erupted all around
as Raz blushed and tried to find a comfortable position.
Finding his footing, Raz glanced up and found Master Dou,
the Master of all Masters, staring right back at him with the
same unsettling, soul-piercing stare he always had.

The look alone was almost enough to make Raz jump
into the river.

The Grand Elder of the Masters of the Celestial Temple looked every bit the part. He sat cross-legged on a wooden platform at the river bank. His long flowing white hair, or what was left of it under his perfectly bald crown, blew gently in the breeze.

Nearly every day, he wore the same faded purple and gold robes. The only piece of his attire one could call ornate was the necklace of metal orbs around his neck. The old face was well hidden under a great bushy beard and mustache that all but hid any sign of emotion. To guess what the 149-year-old elder might be thinking meant looking into his eyes, which Raz found uncomfortable in the extreme. The old Master had a talent for looking through a person, like their secrets were written out for him to see plainly.

And Raz had plenty of secrets - bullies to defeat, Kung

Master
Dou

Fulio carrots to master, botched break-ins and sealed away demons to ignore. Mercifully, Master Dou closed his eyes, and Raz blew out a sigh of relief. It'd been a rough night - he turned over his shoulder to look at Rin, who was probably having as much trouble concentrating as he was.

Nope.

Rin sat perfectly balanced on one hand, eyes closed serenely. He nibbled at a sandwich in the other. There he was, perfectly still and acting as if the night before hadn't happened. He knew Nox was back there, too, somewhere, but best not to poke that bear.

Beads of sweat pooled on Raz's forehead as he tried to focus and sit still. Everyone else made it look so easy. One of Master Dou's favorite nuggets of wisdom was that the pain and the woes of the body were but an illusion. Easy for him to say, he wasn't the one operating on not-enough-sleep and feeling the pain of who knows how many bruises and cuts. He shook with exertion, and it took everything he had not to slip and fall. The carrot wasn't helping, its hefty weight threatening to pull him into the water at any second. Was this the training Klu meant?

The hairs on the back of Raz's head stood up. Someone was watching him. Slowly, he turned his neck and found the source of his discomfort.

Standing on one leg atop the narrowest and highest pole in the river with the stillness of a statue was Nora. The only visible movement was from the two ribbons that tied her pigtails swaying in the breeze. Her green eyes bore into him, and her narrow face twisted into a judgmental scowl.

Nora was the type that always walked with her chin up, shoulders back, and would rather die than be caught unprepared. While she wasn't the biggest or the strongest, she was well-practiced and precise. Raz had seen her alone some nights, practicing a single step in a combat form repeatedly until it was perfect.

In other words, she was a goody two-shoes - a book-smart butt kisser to the Masters. Worse yet, she was a know-it-all, the kind of person who had an answer for everything. Raz couldn't stand know-it-alls. Especially when they were right all the time.

In a previous life Raz would have avoided people like her. Still, the Masters were always assigning Nora to "tutor" him whenever he screwed up, which roughly translated into her being assigned to him indefinitely.

She straightened up ever so slightly in an exaggerated gesture to try to signal for him to do the same. The Masters said that finding posture and alignment would help with one's spiritual energy and whatever. Raz could practically hear her lecturing him in her head.

A wobble of the poll stole his attention away from her judgemental gaze. Waving his arms, he regained his balance and swore. It was like he was the only one struggling today. He found his footing again and closed his eyes to a half squint, trying his best to push the raging current of thoughts from his mind and focus on the present like Master Dou was always telling them.

Be one with the log; the log is you, you ARE the log...

A pebble ricocheted off the back of Raz's head, causing a sharp tap of pain. He turned over his left shoulder and saw Nox and the Cobras chuckling at him. Other chortles of laughter broke out from the other students. They were quickly silenced when Master Dou cleared his throat.

Nox pointed at Raz then passed the finger over his throat. As soon as Raz confirmed that Master Dou's eyes were still closed, he turned towards Nox and gave him the finger. Old habits die hard, even when your future's on the line.

The Moonken Grandmaster grumbled and rose to his feet. "Never forget that physical balance and mental balance are one in the same. Body and mind are one. A weakness in one, spreads to the other." He smiled and hopped silently to the ground.

"Balance," he continued, "In all things. To remind you of this truth, instead of Mantis form training, we will be continuing this exercise after lunch."

The group of students stifled groans as Dou strode away with his hands folded behind him. As soon as the old man was out of sight, the other Moonken started to make a mass exodus, hissing curses and blowing raspberries at the new kid as they trailed off.

Raz closed his eyes again, trying to ignore them and find the sweet spot, balancing perfectly centered on the wooden caber. He rolled his shoulders back and straightened his posture like Nora was always whining at him to do. Admittedly, it felt like he was swaying a little less.

There was another tap at the back of his head. He gritted his teeth and pretended it didn't bother him.

But then there was another tap. And another. He shot a glance back at Nox, who held up four fingers. Nox was keeping score. It seemed that the Red Cobras weren't ready to let them off the hook today.

Diego tapped Bolo, who passed something over to their fearless leader. Smoothing his pompadour, Nox raised his hand. In it was a rather large rock.

Raz gulped and turned on shaky legs to face Nox, trying his best to remember Klu's movements from the night before. He raised the carrot out in front of him.

All right, Klu, let's put your secret weapon to the test...

From above, Nora coughed uncomfortably.

Nox jerked his throwing arm forward. Raz swung the carrot out to counter and was shocked at how much force the vegetable could generate. Much to Raz's satisfaction, the carrot batted the rock away with ease. Unfortunately, the momentum of the swing sent Raz hurtling off the pole and into the water anyway.

He hit the river with a splash and desperately clawed for the surface to find that something was already pulling him up.

Breaching the waterline, he discovered that he'd been rescued by the great orange carrot, now floating peacefully on the water. This was good, because among Raz's many talents, swimming was not among them.

"Hang on, pal! I'm coming!" Rin dived gracefully into the river. He quickly wrapped the carrot under his arm like a life preserver, dragging it and Raz back to dry land. They heaved onto the shore and barely had a chance to catch their breath before three shadows engulfed them.

"You two ain't so smart, are you?" Nox growled as he leered over them.

"What? In general, or compared to you?" Raz taunted between coughs. Nox placed his toes on Raz's forehead and pushed, sending him falling into the sand of the riverbank.

"Don't get cute with me, farm boy," he snarled. "What are you doing here?"

"TRYING to meditate and find balance or whatever, what's it look like?" Raz said, too tired to filter his words.

"Yeah, no crap. But WHY?" Nox barked, his voice booming over the rapids. He looked around to make sure no one was close enough to hear, then lowered his voice. "If I remember right, I gave you losers until tonight to get out of my sight. So what... the friggin' hell... are you doing showing up to Master Dou's class?"

"... We didn't want to get in trouble?" Rin squeaked.

Nox tilted his head, the rusty gears of his brain cranking in a feeble attempt to understand.

"Are you dense, or somethin'? As far as you knuckleheads are concerned, you aren't students here anymore. You're done. Finished," Nox said between gritted teeth.

Raz met Nox's cold stare with his own. "Back off, Nox.

You said we had until sundown. I'm just taking in some final words of wisdom from Master Dou," Raz grunted and rose to his feet.

In a flash, Raz was sent toppling to the ground with a leg sweep. Wood poles creaked all around them as the few remaining students fled the scene - off to mind their own business and not get sucked into the vortex that was Nox's fury.

"Don't think I'm not on to you," Nox snarled. Rin's eyes darted to the ground and he broke out in a cold sweat.

"You two chuckleheads are planning something, I can feel it. But never forget who you're up against. Red Cobras FRICKIN' RULE!" he shouted, crossing his arms to his chest then raising them to the sides in idiotic salute. The Cobras turned to leave.

"Not for long," Raz mumbled and gripped the leaves of

the carrot firmly between his fingers.

Nox stopped dead in his tracks and slowly turned. "What did you just say?" he growled. Raz remained silent. Nox started ambling forward.

"SAY IT AGAIN, FARM BOY!" he raged, raising his fist into the air. Raz thought to swing the carrot to find out just how effective his new weapon was.

Just as Nox was about to swing, a brown flash passed under the three Cobras' knees, knocking them to the ground.

"Enough!" came a stern voice from above.

Moments later, a dainty pair of feet landed silently, with perfect form, in front of Raz. He looked up and saw the shape of two pigtails silhouetted in the sunlight.

"Stay out of this, Nora. This has got nothin' to do with you!" Nox snorted and hopped lithely to his feet. Diego, usually the first to lose his cool, was about to lunge forward when Nora's large boomerang wheeled back around and cracked into the side of his head. The boomerang returned to her hand with timing so perfect it was as if she'd planned it advance.

Raz scoffed. Rin sat there, dumbfounded in wide-eyed admiration.

Show off.

"The Masters forbid acts of unsanctioned violence on the grounds of the monastery. Or did the temple's top fighter," she said, voice oozing with sarcasm, "forget that rule already? Too many blows to the head, maybe?" She poked her finger into Nox's chest.

Nox grumbled, unable to come up with a good comeback. "Bah! Why are you standing up for these losers? If it weren't for them, we'd be doing real training instead of sitting here meditating all day!" Nox complained.

"Meditation IS training, Nox. Like the Masters say, balance is at the core of the Moonken way," she retorted. Raz chuckled. Goody-two-shoes or not, Nora was the only one on Crescent Isle who dared to lecture Nox and get away with it.

"Keep actin' all high and mighty if you want, Anako, but someday real soon, you're finally gonna see things MY way," Nox snarled, and Bolo chuckled along as if by reflex. Nox leaned around Nora and pointed directly at Raz and Rin.

"If you ain't the BEST, then you're WORTHLESS. Remember that," he said, then spat into the dirt as he and the other Cobras walked away.

Once they'd skulked off, Nora dusted off her robes and turned towards Raz and Rin. Raz released the breath he'd been holding and held out a hand to Nora.

"Hey thanks for — "

Nora was no longer smiling. Raz knew that look.

"I'm not talking to you!" Nora looked at Rin before he could argue with her. "Whatever your beef with Nox is, you two better squash it, before I have to get involved! And I REALLY don't want to get involved." Nora ordered as she stomped off toward the Monastery dormitory. Rin turned to Raz in stunned silence.

"Did you SEE that?" Rin squealed. "Nora just made Nox run off with his tail between his legs!"

"So?" Raz replied. He didn't like where this was going.

"Remember how Klu was talking about things happening on their own?" Rin said, still staring at Nora as she walked away. "I think a solution just came to us," Rin stumbled as he ran ahead toward the monastery in pursuit. "Hey Nora! Wait up!"

Western Sanctuary

The Celestial Temple at Crescent Isle is also a Monastery for the Moonken who train there. The temple has stood for several thousand years, and is the last remaining remnant of the Monks of Twilight. Many hidden caverns and sealed off rooms still remain undiscovered within it's walls. Ancient relics and dangerous artifacts are stored within the vaults underneath the central structure, but access to these vaults is extremely

Limited. In fact only a few of the masters even know the way through the subteranean maze within the island upon which it's carved.

The temple itself consists of several hundred rooms and was clearly designed to house thousands. However, much of what remains is used for the small number of remaining orphan Moonken quarters, training grounds and libraries.

CHAPTER 9
THE FURY OF NORA ANAKO

"**Y**ou did WHAT?!" Nora screamed, causing every board in the cramped dormitory to shake.

"Shhh! Not so loud!" Raz scolded. He pulled a dry shirt over his head and shot a glance at Rin. "See? I told you this was a bad idea."

Rin shrugged. The ninja boy's friendship with Nora had clouded his judgment. Telling her was a mistake, a big mistake.

"You broke into the Monastery after dark? Then into Klu's…? Hold on! There were magical items under Klu's dojo?!" Nora raved deliriously, pacing the length of the room.

"Wait." She stopped and looked them both over incredulously, "Did you say a DARKSPRITE? YOU FOUGHT AN ACTUAL, BREATHING

DARKSPRITE?!"

"It was," Raz coughed, "only a little one…"

"Are you INSANE?!" she demanded, ignoring Raz and turning her attention to Rin, who tried to melt into the shadows.   "If Master Klu didn't show up you could've gotten yourself killed!"

"Hey! Lay off of him!" Raz interjected. "It's not our fault Klu was keeping ANCIENT DEMONS hidden away under the dojo. If you ask me, I think we did an excellent job of softening that ol' Darksprite up for the old man…"

"And YOU!" Nora snapped, wheeling towards Raz like an angry shark on the scent of blood. "Don't think for a second, that I'm fooled by your moronic tough guy act. You can barely stand on one leg without hurting yourself somehow."

"Uh-huh," Raz grunted, "and how many Darksprites has Miss Goody-Two-Shoes helped take down lately?"

In retaliation, Nora poked at one of Raz's many visible bruises, causing him to wince and collapse backward onto his bed.

"At least I didn't throw myself into a river with... with..." she trailed off and pointed, "with WHATEVER in Speria that is."

Raz followed the direction of her finger to the fifty-pound behemoth of a carrot, which leaned inconspicuously against the wall next to Raz's bed.

"It's a carrot," he replied calmly.

"I can see it's a carrot, you idiot! But WHY are you lugging it around everywhere?!"

"It's uh... the secret to Kung Fulio?" Raz replied honestly.

"URGH! You are INFURIATING, you know that?" she shouted at Raz. "Know what you are? A bad influence!"

"You saying this is MY fault? He practically dragged me into it!" Raz countered, gesturing at Rin.

"Whatever do you mean?" Rin asked innocently. "It's only natural that two super best friends would help each other out when the goin' gets tough."

"It's what you might call an... uneasy alliance," Raz chimed in quickly. Rin scrunched his nose at this less-than-stellar description of their friendship.

"I can't believe you two did something so... so... completely stupid, just because Nox was giving you a hard time. That's just what he does."

"A hard time?!" Raz spat back. "Maybe you misheard. Nox isn't just being his usual kind of an A-hole, he's kicking us out of town. TO-DAY."

"It's true! That's why he went after us after Master Dou's meditation," Rin protested.

Nora scrunched up her nose and shook her head. "Nox? Running Moonken off the island? You actually expect me to believe that bull-hooey?"

Raz paused mid-way through changing out of his wet pants and stared at Nora incredulously. "Hold up. So you've got no problems accepting that me and Rin took on a Darksprite, but somehow Nox and the Red Cobras being colossal douchebags is the part you DON'T believe?!"

"Come on, that's not fair," Nora whined. "Nox gives me a hard time, too, you know!"

Silence.

Raz and Rin looked at each other and then rolled their eyes. Nora darted her attention back and forth between them, suddenly feeling unbalanced at this united front against her dignity.

"W-What?!" Nora sputtered defensively. "Didn't you see the other day when he threw that soup on me at lunch? Or... when he made fun of my Tiger Form in front of Master Yobei?"

Rin stayed silent. Raz suspected the big guy probably had a few stories of abuse at Nox's hands that could blow her out of the water.

"Gee whiz, Nora, he spilled a whole SOUP on you? I never realized you had it so rough," Raz replied, pushing out his lower lip in a child-like pout. "Bet it took a while to get those stains out..."

"Shut up, Raz," she grunted, flushing red.

"Listen, Nora," Raz continued with a sigh, "Nox doesn't bug you because you're the Monastery's golden child, the Master's favorite. Even the older kids look up to you." Nora squirmed in discomfort as Raz heaped on the praise. "It's a bit of a different story for guys like us."

"Th-That's not true! Pft. Golden Child, I..." Even though she denied it, she rather liked the idea of being thought of as the star student. She rambled on denying the accusation as she met Rin's honest gaze.

"Nora, he's got a point," he said plainly. It was enough, she didn't resume her argument.

"Okay, fine, I admit, the Cobras can get a little... rough," she conceded, wincing as she examined Raz's bruises. "And yeah, they have NO respect for the Master's

rules. But surely you
guys must have done
something to piss them
off."

"Not really,
no," Raz grunted.
"Apparently, Nox
thinks we're in the way
around here. He just
wants us out of the
picture entirely."

"He's…" She
snapped her fingers as
if she'd stumbled onto
a great epiphany, "He's
probably just trying
to scare you, that's
all! There's no way

he could do something so blatantly against the rules. The
Masters would never allow it," Nora said, chin up proudly as
if she'd won.

Raz and Rin looked at each other and raised their
eyebrows incredulously. Nora's unbending conviction that
the Celestial Temple rules were absolute reminded Raz of a
naive child's belief that the moon was made of cheese. It just
wasn't reality.

This time it was Rin who spoke up first, much to Raz's
surprise. "What do you think happened to Kareena?" he
said.　Nora stopped in her tracks and blinked at him in
confusion. Raz stayed silent, the name didn't ring a bell.

"What do you mean? She said she was going on a
vacation to visit her Earthfather," she replied.

"For six months? Nope. It was the Cobras, Nora," Rin
said, shaking his head. "And before that. You remember that
other kid, Tong? The kid with the stutter?"

Nora gulped and nodded her head, but said nothing.

"That whole story about how he 'ran away'? It was bull. Nox just got sick of listening to him, and kicked him out, too," Rin continued.

Raz chimed in, "If you're not the best, then you're worthless. Isn't that what he said?"

Nora's eyes went wide as the truth started to sink in, the fragments of rumors and stories she'd heard coalescing into a horrible reality. She started pacing, shaking her head furiously like a snowglobe, as if by refusing to let the thoughts settle, it would stop them from being real.

"No way. It can't be... I mean, I remember Kareena mentioning something about Nox, but I would have known," she mumbled.

"Everyone knows, Nora. Probably even the Masters," Rin said. Raz sat leaning against the dresser, quietly impressed that Rin had managed to find a chink in Nora's perfect-student armor.

"... What are you two going to do? What's your plan?" she finally asked.

"We're working on it," Raz said, pointing at the carrot as if that would explain everything. "Plus, when have you ever known me to have a plan?"

"So, why tell me?" she asked.

Rin's smile widened as Raz's frown deepened. This was the moment that Rin had been waiting for.

"Well, y' see, while we're waiting for Raz's carrot to, erm, *do whatever it's supposed to do*, we thought maybe we could get a little... help?" he asked. Nora remained silent until she realized what he was hinting at. Her eyes went wide.

"No. Wait a minute. No, no, no, no, no! You didn't think I would actually help you fight the Cobras?! Are you crazy?!" she exclaimed, throwing her hands wildly into the air.

"Well, we saw how you handled him at the river and

thought—"

"Oooooh, but of course!" Nora cut Rin off. "Let me just drop everything, disobey the Masters, and join up with the worst couple of klutzes I've ever met so I can wage war on a ferocious gang of miscreants!"

"Careful Nora, you're getting sarcasm all over Rin's sheets. I heard that junk's contagious," Raz said, rolling his eyes. "See, Rin? I TOLD you she'd be like this!"

"Be like WHAT, exactly?" she fired back.

"THIS! The same way you always are! I didn't even want to tell you about any of this!"

"Why not?!" she demanded, placing her hands on her hips defiantly.

"Because you're doing what you always do, Nora! You know, you may be book-smart and know way more history, and battle tactics, and numbers," Raz grit his teeth, "AND you may be liked by just about everyone at the Monastery. But your ability to read a room? Your empathy? It SUCKS!"

She scrunched up her nose and threw her chin back to avoid Raz's gaze. "What's that supposed to mean?"

"It means that if taking down Nox got you a little merit badge with the Masters, you'd do it. But when your so-called friends are in trouble, Nox and his goons may as well not even exist!"

"Th-That's not true!" she stammered, her face bright red. "Just because I don't want to get dragged into your problems doesn't mean I don't care!"

"Is that so? Well, I hope that's true, because come sundown, we might not be here to drag you down anymore!" Raz growled.

It was creeping up to midday now, and this detour was costing valuable time. Tension filled the air like noxious fumes. Rin tried to place himself between Raz and Nora as the two stubborn Moonken stewed in silence. Nora squared herself back with Raz and was about to open her mouth to renew her verbal assault when she was interrupted by a loud bang at the windowpane.

A huge black bird pecked at the glass furiously to get their attention. There was some kind of scroll attached by a metal clip on its neck.

"Move over," Nora grunted and shoved Raz aside. She pet the bird's head gently as she carefully untied the scroll and began to read. The bird cawed noisily then flew away as Raz and Rin stared in confused silence.

"What's it say?" Rin asked, unable to contain his curiosity.   She said nothing, her eyes scanning the page over and over nervously.

After a brief silence, and with worry in her eyes, she nervously spoke. "I've got to go!" she said and darted for the door.   Rin slid in front of her and blocked her path. "Wait! Where are you going?" he squeaked.

"Something's going down at Jubee's. He needs my help," she replied.

"Jubee? That old guy that runs the Bed and Breakfast outside of town?" Rin asked suspiciously. "Always thought there was something's fishy about that guy," He smirked, knowing very well that Jubee was a Barakewdo. Their species were descendants of the sea, but those who turned away from their kind prided themselves on wearing disguises to fit in with the rest of society.

"Seriously? Now's not the time for jokes."

"But—"

"Now, if you'll excuse me," she tried to squeeze past him. "I'm in a hurry." But the big guy threw out his arms and stopped her again.

"Hold up! You're just gonna leave?! But... WE need your help!" Rin pleaded.

Nora tried to dodge and get around him, but even compared to Nora, Rin could be shockingly quick.

"Your buddy," Nora said, throwing a searing glance at

Raz, "made it perfectly clear that you don't want my help!"

Raz returned the gesture by giving her the finger over Rin's shoulder as soon as she looked away.

"Who? Raz?" Rin asked innocently. "He's just a little... passionate sometimes," he said as he smacked Raz's hand away. "He didn't mean it. Did ya, Raz?"

Raz folded his arms and grumbled moodily under his breath in response.

"See?" Rin plowed ahead. "He's totally down for teaming up. Trust me, he's a really great guy when you give him a chance."

Nora's eyes darted from Rin, to the door, to Raz. She was trapped.

"Rin, come on! I'm not joking around! I think Jubee's really in trouble," she said, growing increasingly more anxious.

"So are WE! Don't you care that Nox is gonna kick us out?" Rin said. Raz watched with mild amusement from a distance as Nora squirmed.

"Of course I care," she countered. "But what do you want me to do? I can't just go around beating up other students for you!"

"Yeah... well... maybe you can talk to him! Nox at least listens to you!" Rin said, to which Raz guffawed loudly.

Talk to Nox, that's a good one.

Nora looked at the window impatiently, and saw storm clouds gathering on the horizon.

"FINE!" she conceded, and sighed heavily. "I'll help you." Rin pumped his fist in victory.

"On ONE condition," she added quickly before he could get too carried away. "The Masters say that one side of a bridge is only as strong as the other."

Raz rolled his eyes. "What's your point?"

"That if you want me to help you, you've got to help me first," she explained, turning to Raz, who picked at a nail absentmindedly.

"With Jubee? Sure, whatever. No problem."

"I mean it," Nora said, gathering up her boomerang and slinging it over her shoulder. "If you don't take my problems seriously, why should I bother with yours?"

"Don't worry, Nora! You can count on us! Team RiRaz to the rescue!" Rin declared and saluted.

"Team Ri... Raz? Did you really smash your names together into one? Jeez, you guys are such dorks..." Nora sighed and headed for the door with Rin trailing enthusiastically behind. Just as she was about to leave, Nora poked her head back through the door and looked at Raz.

"And Raz, don't forget your carrot." she insisted. He shrugged and patted its rough surface.

"Well, according to Master Klu, it IS the secret to Kung Fulio," he replied with a wry smile.

CHAPTER 10
BETWEEN LIGHT AND SHADOW

Raziel's arms felt like heavy noodles. After an hour of walking the forest trail with the carrot slung over his shoulder, Klu's words rattled in his mind endlessly. It couldn't just be any old carrot. But what was the secret? What was he missing?

Now, Raz was beginning to wonder if the giant vegetable wasn't just the spacey Master's idea of a joke. A passive-aggressive way to pack him some food for his exile, perhaps? He could just imagine the Masters having a good laugh about this one.

Nora and Rin forged on ahead further up the trail, old buddies, occasionally pausing to turn back and snicker at him.   Maybe they had been in on it too.

Bun-Buns twitched their noses and scurried away into the bushes ahead of him. Raz briefly considered doing the

same. Maybe he could live among the little creatures. The giant carrot would undoubtedly be a valuable bargaining chip to enter Bun-Bun society.

"Hey, Raz," Rin muttered, trying to hold back a chuckle.

Annoyed, Raz replied. "What?"

"What's a vegetable's favorite martial art?"

Raz sighed, figuring it would make it slightly less painful to play along. It was like pulling out a splinter. Better to get it over with quickly.

"I don't know. What?"

Rin flattened his two hands and chopped at the air enthusiastically. "CARROT-tee! Hai YA!" he exclaimed then burst out laughing at his own joke.

Raz groaned. There was a muffled snort up the path. Raz snapped his head towards Nora, but by then, she'd already regained her composure, hiding any traces of laughter with a suspicious-looking yawn.

"Come on, Rin, give me a break! I'm in enough pain as it is," Raz whined and adjusted the weight of the carrot. He wasn't sure how many carrot jokes there were in Speria but he started to think he might hear them all before the day was through.

"Hey… hey Raz," Rin started again. It was clear that

he'd come up with another one. At this point, he wasn't sure what was worse: getting kicked off of Crescent Isle or suffering through more jokes.

"Why's a carrot make a good ninja assassin?" he asked. Raz stopped walking and stretched out his aching legs.

"No. Please, not another one. I will pay you not to tell me another stupid carrot joke," Raz pleaded.

"Hey, Raz, what's the hold up? We're already running late!" Nora called out and walked towards them.

"I don't care!" Raz protested. Nora and Rin looked at each other, and the hint of a smile cracked on Nora's lips.

"Don't care, huh?" she said in mock sympathy. "Would you say that you don't... CAR-ROT all?!" she asked and her and Rin howled with laughter, leaning on each other for support.

"Ugh, I thought dealing with only one Rin was bad enough. Now he's got an echo," Raz complained. They composed themselves as best they could, occasionally snorting and convulsing uncontrollably.

"Call it... character building," she said. Then, as if a switch was flicked, her icy-cool composure returned. "Now come on, fun's over. We're almost there."

Finally, the weight of the carrot, both physically and mentally, had reached a breaking point. Raz slung it off his shoulders and slammed it down into the dirt.

"Nope! We've been pelting it out of Crescent Isle with no break. I'm not going another step until you tell us what we've gotten into."

Nora frowned and looked up as a patch of clouds passed over the sun through the trees.

"Fine. We can take a little rest. But just until this rain passes," she said, slinging her boomerang off her shoulder.

"Rain? What rain?" Raz asked. Nora took out a small umbrella and unfurled it. At that exact moment, thunder cracked above and the rain came down as if she'd planned it.

She smiled at him smugly.

They hustled over to a sheltered spot just off the path. Raz upended the carrot into a makeshift bench and Nora brushed off a nearby rock before sitting down.

"Oooh! Perfect timing! I was in the mood for a snack!" Rin chipped in. "Maybe some carr—"

"Not. Another. Word," Raz threatened. Rin chuckled to himself and rummaged around in his impossibly stuffed satchel, producing three plates and some apples. He cut the apples into slices and passed them around.

Raz plopped his butt on the carrot and scooched over so Rin could do the same.

"So," Rin said, breaking the silence, "don't leave us in suspense, Nora. What's got ol' Jubee's gills in a twist?"

If anyone else made that kind of joke, Nora would probably give them one of her famous icy stares and scold them, but she was remarkably tolerant of Rin's antics.

"Beats me. He was kinda vague," she sighed and drew out Jubee's scroll from her robe. "Here, see for yourself."

She tossed Rin the scroll, but with no hands free, he juggled it with his feet to keep it off the ground. Raz snatched the scroll out of the air and unfurled it in front of him.

"Ahem… 'Nora. Got some trouble heeeruuughhh,'" he read aloud. "Not very descriptive, is he?"

Rin grabbed the scroll and analyzed it skeptically. "Wait… did he actually take the time to write ""heeeruuugh?""

"That's what it says!" Nora shrugged. "For all I know he's just got a bad rush of customers or got in a big shipment

or something," she said. Raz grabbed the scroll and rolled
it up. "Somehow, I doubt you'd want backup for that," he
reasoned.

A frown spread to her face as she looked around the
silent trees. It was as if something was watching her from the
gloom. "I don't know, I've got a bad feeling. Call it intuition.
Something doesn't feel right out here."

"Since when are you and Jubee best buds?" Rin
questioned, raising an eyebrow in suspicion.

"I..." she hesitated, as if she were about to tell a
deep dark secret. "I've been helping out in his shop on the
weekends."

Raz and Rin looked at each other in disbelief. The
thought of Nora smiling sweetly, serving customers, and
restocking shelves was difficult to picture. Stern and serious
Nora, always taking the monastery so seriously, slaving
away for a few extra coins. It was too much. Raz burst out
laughing.

"What? What's so funny?" she demanded, tipping
her umbrella forward to hide her quickly reddening face.
Rin glanced over and grinned as if he'd read Raz's mind.
Suddenly, he sat straight-backed and stared at Nora from
over his nose.

"Oh, girl!" he commanded in his most elegant and most
refined accent. "Could you fetch me a spot of Jinji balm? I
have the most terrible rash on my backside!"

"Oh yes!" Raz chimed in, sporting his best impression
of a foppish big-city human. "No, no, no! Not that hogwash!
The good stuff, girl, the good stuff!"

"And be snappy!" Rin picked up a stick and slammed
it down on the ground as if it were a jewel-encrusted cane
and turned to Raz. He twiddled the ends of his invisible
mustache.   "These little Moonken
think that we all live as long as they do! I daresay we'll be
dead by the time she finds it."

"Yes! Quite!" Raz replied in mock indignation.

Raz and Rin burst out laughing, clutching at their sides. The umbrella had abandoned its purpose of keeping Nora dry and instead served to hide her embarrassment.

"Sh-Shut up!" Nora protested. She moved the umbrella aside and threw a piece of apple at Rin in retaliation. Rin moved his mouth to intercept and caught it between his teeth.

"Gross," she muttered.

"I think 'impressive' is the word you're looking for," he said as he devoured all but the core of the fruit. She couldn't help but crack a smile. After Raz stopped giggling, he tossed the scroll back to Nora. She caught it and carefully put it away.

"I'm not sure how I feel about this new alliance of yours." She shot a suspicious look at both of them. "So far, it's caused me nothing but trouble."

"Not YOUR alliance," Rin corrected. "OUR alliance."

Raz nodded in agreement. "That's right. We're not just here out of the kindness of our hearts, remember?"

Nora shifted uncomfortably as she remembered her hastily made deal. "I remember. I just… I've been wanting to talk to you guys about that. What exactly do you expect me to do?"

"There's not much to it, really. Nox and his cronies are gunning for us, so you're going to help us fight 'em off," Raz explained.

"I already told you, I'm not going to help you pick a fight with the Cobras!" she protested.

"We're not picking a fight with them, per say," Rin said, trying to mediate the rising tension, "it's self-defense."

"Exactly. Nox started this fight, not us," Raz agreed and handed his empty fruit plate to Rin.

"It doesn't matter who started it. Don't you guys listen to the Master's lessons?" Nora asked.

Oh goody. Here we go… Raz thought as he rolled his eyes.

"Sure," Raz said, "ride the cosmic waves, be one with the universe, flow like water, et cetera, et cetera. I got it." He recoiled as a piece of apple hit him right on the forehead.

"No, dummy!" Nora squawked. "I'm talking about causality."

The blank, confused expression on both of their faces made it clear that they were entirely in the dark.

"Master Dou says that when two swords clash, it dulls BOTH blades."

"Meaning...?" Raz groaned and wiped the juice off his forehead.

"That when two sides use violence, it weakens them both. And everyone else, for that matter. You're just fighting to save your own hide, and that'll have consequences. Master Dou says, the energy of the cosmos merely echoes whatever it is that you send out," she explained.

"Yeah, that's great and all, but I don't think Nox is pondering the mysteries of the universe when he's punching our lights out," Raz reasoned.

"He's right. Nox isn't really the philosophical type," Rin agreed.

"How'd a jerk like him get to be top dog on the island anyway?" Raz asked. "Why's everyone so afraid of him?"

Nora thought for a moment. "I'm not sure they're afraid of him, per se, but he is a very skilled fighter. It all started a few years ago. Word got out that he'd somehow managed to beat Master Yibada in a fight using some sort of SECRET move. A few days later, Yibada was gone. Nobody's seen or heard from him since."

Raz knew the name. Everyone on Crescent Isle did. Yibada, the only non-Moonken Master of the monastery. A warrior so skilled he had earned his place through combat alone.

That really grabbed Raz's attention. "Nox beat him? No

way! But… he's just another kid! A trainee!" He stumbled, puzzled at how such a thing could be possible.

"I know, right?" Nora agreed, taking another bite. "But anytime someone asked the Circle of Elders about Yibada, they kept silent. Not a peep! Next thing you know, kids are lining up in droves outside of Nox's room to learn about this secret move he invented."

Nora bunched her free hand into a fist, clearly enraged.

"Then Bolo and Diego joined up with him, and they made themselves new uniforms… and then they start calling themselves that STUPID name. Before you know, it that punk had started up a school of his own, right under the Master's noses! It's an affront to the dignity of the monastery!" She slammed her fist into her palm.

Raz shook his head. Leave it to Nora to find the least remarkable thing about Nox to take the most offense to.

"So…" Raz cut in, "What's this secret power move of his?"

"That's just it! No one knows! It's probably not even a real thing! But that doesn't even matter. What matters is that people believe it."

"Sounds like a load of B.S. to me," Raz said.

"It's clearly grade-A bull," Nora said bitterly. "He believes that he's returning the strength of the ancients to the Moonken again. And the people who follow him? They don't just believe it, it's like a religion or something."

"Why?"

"I guess it struck a chord with the people on the island. They don't understand the Masters. They think they're too soft - too passive."

Raz puckered his lip in agreement. "Are they wrong? I mean… Moonken are the Masters of the ancient art of Kung Fulio, But we sit around on our butts all day while terrible stuff happens everywhere."

"Kung Fulio?" Nora questioned. "Oh, you've been

listening to Master Klu again haven't you?"

Raz looked puzzled. "Wait... what do you mean? Moonken are the only ones who can tap into the power of Kung Fulio. We're supposed to use it to fight the bad guys! Isn't that our whole purpose? The reason we're constantly in training?"

Nora rolled her eyes. Despite all of her respect for the council, it seemed that there was indeed a line. When it came to the sleepy-eyed old hermit, she made an exception. "Master Klu has his own way of dealing with his past. Kung Fulio? Good guys and bad guys? Those are all just made up words."

Raz's face scrunched. He couldn't accept it. "Made-up!? What are you talking about? Why else would we be training every day if NOT to fight the bad guys!?"

Nora took a deep breath. "Oh? And who exactly decides who's bad and who's good?"

Rin's eyes darted back and forth between Raz and Nora like a spectator at a sporting event. One got the sense he was enjoying himself, or at the very least, enjoying the two of them interacting without shouting for a change.

"Doesn't the Monastery dispatch monks all the time to go settle conflicts all over Speria, though?" Raz asked.

"They do, but they're committed only to maintaining balance in Speria through their presence. They don't take sides in local scuffs, or politics, or anything like that."

"Or against a jerk student and his little gang," Rin added helpfully, holding up his little plate to the rain to rinse it off before putting it away in his bag.

"Of course not," Nora said like it was the most natural thing in the world. "Why would they react differently to one bad apple on Crescent Isle than they do anywhere else?"

"Then what's the point of sending them out at all?" Raz mumbled. "You know how bad things are getting outside of Crescent Isle. Seems to me that the Masters could DO something about it if they wanted to."

"But think about it!" Nora said in that tone that stank of a lecture. "Do you remember that incident with the gang war in Belgarde six months ago? In the end, Master Dou decided to withdraw the monks from the city. The resulting bloodshed left a lot of people questioning if he was fit to lead the monastery."

"That's exactly what I'm saying! Why didn't the Masters help them? They could've squashed both sides!" Raz shouted passionately.

"Because helping comes with a cost, Raz," Nora lectured sternly. "It's not as simple as taking out a few gang leaders. To really put a stop to it, you'd have to wipe out both gangs entirely. Think of all the destruction it would have caused, the lives lost! Does that sound like helping to you?"

"I guess not," Raz admitted reluctantly. "Still, a lot of innocent people died, anyway. And half the stuff you said were, whatcha call 'ems...? Hypotheticals! They should have at least TRIED to help."

"Yeah, Nox said that too," Nora said, looking down her nose at him. Raz didn't like where this was headed.

"The fact is," she elaborated, "a lot of people around here insist that our kind should use our strength to fix the problems of the world and shape it - to FORCE warring nations into peace.   That's how they interpret the Moonken belief of finding balance. Balance through force."

"Master Dou does love to drone on about

'balance'..." Raz observed.

Nora was so worked up that she didn't notice.

"Balance isn't just a word, it's a belief. In all things, there is balance. A lot of times, it means doing nothing at all. Getting involved in other people's messes only creates more problems for them - and for you."

"Huh?" Raz tilted his neck to the side.

"Ugh, you are dense. It's like this," she hopped down from the rock. In the mud, she drew a crude representation of a see-saw with the tip of her umbrella. On top of the see-saw she drew a big circle.

"See, imagine this ball is Speria and every living thing in it. There it sits right in the middle - Chaos and Order equally balanced on either side," then she drew a big stick figure with horns on one side. "and the closer anything is to it, the more it teeters."

"Right! And that's where we're supposed to come in, to balance stuff out. Right?" Raz interjected as he grabbed the stick and drew Moonken stick figures on the other side. Nora grunted.

"The problem is that if Moonken get involved in EVERY conflict, we'd be applying force, a force that disrupts the balance of yet another system." Nora violently scribbled out arrows from the Moonken side of the scale, pointing towards the center. "If Moonken came in and solved every problem, no one would learn how to solve their own problems. The world wouldn't grow or get any better, it'd descend into CHAOS," she exclaimed and scribbled the ball of Speria out. "They'd only expect us to fix everything - and start blaming us when anything goes wrong."

Rin chimed in. "Yeah, everything from stopping wars, to getting your cat down from a tree,"

"Exactly," Nora agreed.

"So you're saying that 'balance' just means sitting back and doing nothing?" Raz summarized.

"Sometimes. Yes. Master Dou teaches us not to look at the black of night, or the light of day, but the gray… right there in the moments of twilight. The true balance of the universe rests in the space between light and shadow."

"How very poetic," Raz commented dryly, throwing out a polite, but mocking slow clap as he did. "Ya know, at the end of the day, all that talk about the nature of chaos and order sounds nice, but I doubt it does much to help a family being murdered by gangsters in Belgarde, or people trying to escape all the other injustice in the world. Sometimes right is right and wrong is wrong." Raz had a determined look of defiance in his eye that worried her. "Someone needs to do something."

"And you're starting to sound just like him," Nora said.

"What? Nox? No way. He wants to instill strength through fear," Raz observed.

"Yeah! That's right," Rin chimed in. "Nox is always raving about how he's got these big plans to make the monastery strong again. But if he got his way, he'd have Moonken out fighting all over Speria."

Nora poked him to continue that line of thinking, "Which would…?"

Raz continued the thought. "Make them blame us for their war."

They were both thinking it, but Rin said it first: "It would turn all of Speria against us."

The words hit them both like a train. Their faces went white and they turned towards each other.

"Didn't Nox mention that something big was about to go down?" Rin confirmed. "Do you think that's what he meant?"

"Sounds to me like Nox is a ticking time bomb, and even the Masters are set on ignoring him until it's too late," Raz countered.

He turned to Nora. "Now you see why we have to do

something about him?"

She blinked as sunlight broke through the trees and washed over her face. She stared off into the distance, her mind lost in the past.

"He wasn't always so big-headed," she said. "You might not believe this, but years ago when he first came here, he was pretty nice. You probably won't believe me, but he cares more about the future of the Moonken than anyone I've ever met. I don't know what he's got planned. But if Nox is up to something, there's got to be more to it than you think."

"So does that make it all okay? The Red Cobras? Him choosing who gets to stay and who goes on Crescent Isle?" Raz retorted.

"No," she admitted quietly.

Raz was about to respond when they heard a loud crack in the distance. A flock of birds passed noisily overhead. The three Moonken stood up and looked up - nothing but blue sky.

"Thunder? I thought the storm passed us already," Rin mused and scratched his head.

KAPOW!

It sounded again. Nora and Rin looked up at the clear sky for signs of a storm, but not Raz. He knew that sound, and it sure wasn't thunder. He snapped his fingers to get Nora's attention then pointed in the direction of the sound.

"Is that the direction of Jubee's by chance?" Raz asked, dragging the carrot as he moved back to the path. Nora nodded, immediately on edge at Raz's sudden determination. He forged ahead as Rin and Nora struggled to catch up.

"Hey! Slow down! You're not supposed to run on a full stomach!" Rin called out.

"Yeah, you were the one who was whining about taking a break. Why the hurry all the sudden?" Nora demanded.

Raz paused and turned back. "That wasn't thunder. That was a gunshot. Something bad's going down at Jubee's," Raz said and hefted the carrot onto his shoulder.

CHAPTER 11
A TEST OF SKILL

A sign hung above the entrance to the curved walkway leading down into the bay. Engraved in the wooden plank, it read:

WELCOME TRAVELLER, PEACE AND SOLITUDE AWAIT YOU.

It's worth noting that this sign was currently full of bullet holes and partially on fire as Raz, Nora, and Rin slid to stop underneath it, gasping and panting to try and catch their breath.

"Is this," Raz paused and gasped for air, throwing the colossal carrot off his back, "Is this it?"

KRA-KOW!

The gunshot rang out around the corner, just out of sight from where the three Moonken trainees stood. They watched, mouths agape, as a screaming man in nothing but

his boxer shorts ran toward them, his eyes wide in abject
terror.

"THE PLANTS! THE PLAAAAAAAAAAAANTS!"
he cried as he ran past, a pair of trousers gripped tightly in
his fist.

Suffice it to say, this was unusual behavior for a guest
leaving the idyllic comforts of Jubee's Rock House.

They dashed along the wooden terrace which
wrapped around the back of the massive stones from which
the inn was carved. They were almost at the stairs that led
down to the bay and the beachfront when an unnatural
green shape caught Raz's attention. He put on the brakes
and skidded to a halt at the top of the stairs, stopping so
suddenly that Nora and Rin nearly bowled him over.

It was a good thing they didn't, or Raz's story might
have been over right then and there.

"What is it? Why'd you stop?" Nora asked between
breaths. As an explanation, Raz simply pointed at the sight
down the stairs.

The narrow beach that housed the general store and the inn's entrance was half-covered in a writhing mass of spiky vines. They swarmed around themselves as if they were alive, and growing at an unnatural rate. The vines had almost completely engulfed the small hut at the far end of the beach where Jubee ran the general store, and slithered along the beach like probing fingers. They ran across the various tables of goods and up the front of the inn that walled in the bay.

Nearly everywhere he looked, Raz could see groups of small wooden creatures giggling and laughing as they tore apart and smashed the contents of Jubee's general store. Dozens of them. The tiny round bodies resembled coconuts with nubby legs, their gleeful faces nothing more than holes on their hollow bodies. Each one had a unique flower or leaf springing from the top of its head.

A group of them played tug of war with a shovel that ended with the tool snapping in half. Both sides laughed hysterically and shot off looking for their next plaything. On the table where Jubee normally set up his ointments and medicines, the tiny fat seedlings had set up an impromptu can-can line, joyously kicking the contents onto the sand.

On the inn's roof, a whole line of them sat, swinging their stubby little legs as they sung a happy song in their squeaky voices. A couple of them wiggled their tiny wooden

butt cheeks and blew raspberries at the Moonken with nauseating playful defiance.

One could be forgiven at first glance for thinking they were cute. But they were anything but.

They hummed in unison. In response, the vines slithered around them, and spread out further along the sand and up the walls. It wouldn't be long before both the beach and the inn were completely overgrown.

"Iroko Minions? What are they doing here?!" Nora wondered, "Where's Jubee?"

The Barrakewdo proprietor of the inn was nowhere to be seen.

Raz had encountered Iroko Minions once before after arriving at Crescent Isle, but never this many at once. The Masters had taken him and a few other students out to help the local farmers when a few of the little suckers ran amok. Iroko Minions were dangerous creatures wrapped in an adorable little package. It was all fun and games until they started gnawing at your heels, or wrapping vines around your throat.

"Help!" A muffled shout caught Raz's attention from somewhere above the walkway. He looked up and saw a young boy staring down at him through a back window of the inn. He looked terrified.

Raz adjusted the carrot on his shoulder. "Whatever this thing is good for, I hope it kicks in soon. Cuz I think I'm gonna to need it."

The moment he started moving down the steps, a hand seized his collar.

"ERK!" Raz choked as he was roughly jerked backward.

"Wait!" Nora shouted, then released her grip on his robe as if she hadn't realized she'd done it. "What are you doing?!"

"What am I doing? What are YOU doing?!" he shot

back accusingly. "Jubee — and who-knows-how-many other people are trapped down there! I'm gonna DO something!"

A flash of uncertainty crossed Nora's face as she looked around her, but then she threw back her shoulders and blocked his path.

"I can't allow it," she said sternly with the slightest shake in her voice. "Those are Iroko Minions. We are NOT authorized to engage Storm Shadows on our own."

Raz merely gestured to the chaos behind her. "And what are we supposed to do? Just sit here with our thumbs up our butts while these little monsters tear the place apart?!"

Nora's eyes darted back and forth with uncertainty. "We need to go back to Crescent Isle and get the Masters!"

Raz grit his teeth.

"This isn't one of those times when you can sit back and wait for the universe to balance itself out! You go and do whatever you need to, Nora. But I'm not going anywhere," he resolved firmly.

"The heck does that mean!? Raz, this isn't a game! Storm Shadows are bad news! You'd be nuts to try and fight them alone!" Nora protested.

Raz looked over her shoulder at the slithering vines amassing on the beach all around them, then flopped the carrot back over his shoulder, readying his body for combat.

"Wouldn't be the craziest thing I've done today," Raz said. He smirked and gave her a nod. "But by the time you get to Crescent Isle and back, I'll have this whole mess wrapped up in a tidy bow for ya."

Nora's mouth twitched as she struggled in vain to form a reply.

Raz put his hand on Nora's shoulder and gently moved her aside. Rin looked back and forth between the both of them, then ran after Raz giving her an apologetic shrug as he trotted off.

Nora was speechless. Two of the worst students in the monastery were about to get themselves killed by Storm Shadows, on her watch. She closed her eyes, gritted her teeth, and swore under her breath. That wouldn't float too well with the Masters, and she knew it. She reached behind her back and unlatched the fastener, gripping the handle of her boomerang.

Raz and Rin slid to a stop at the bottom of the stairs. They heard a shrill battle cry from above.

"Neeee heeeeeeeeee!"

An Iroko Minion wearing a glass jar as a helmet hurtled down at them with a kitchen knife in one hand and a pot lid in the other. Moments before impact, there was a deafening crack. The jar exploded, and the Iroko went flying.

Across the beach, sticking out from the top of a large wooden barrel, was the smoking business end of a shotgun.

"I think we found ol' fish face..." Rin muttered.

"You think?" Raz replied with oozing sarcasm.

"Hey now! Who ya callin' fish face, pointy ears?!" Jubee yelled, and raised his head above the lid of the barrel. The Barrakewdo's otherwise fish-like features were covered rather obviously with a set of thick glasses and a gray strap-on beard. This was Jubee's blatant attempt to appear more human. The few Barrakewdos who escaped the southern

spires were masters of disguise. But the twang in Jubee's voice was unmistakable.

"If y'all came to cause more trouble, yer gonna find yerself blasted to smithereens along with them l'il wooden devils!" he cried, and inserted another shell.

"Whoa, whoa, whoa! Don't shoot! It's me! It's Nora!" Nora called back, waving her hands above her head.

"Nora?!" Jubee called out suspiciously and pulled down the thick glasses to get a better look. "It's 'bout time you showed up! Who're yer friends?"

"We're her backup!" Rin proclaimed with his arms crossed and his chest out. Before she could debate this, Nora squeaked, ducking just in time to avoid a can of soup hurtling at her face. Raz kicked a table over and all three Moonken crouched behind it for cover.

"Jubee, we need to get you out of here!" Nora called

out.   Jubee leaned out the barrel, spat into the sand, and blasted another group of the forest sprites that had been trying to climb into the inn.

"No can do, kiddo! This here's ma home!" Jubee declared. He adjusted his fake beard, and snapped the shotgun apart to load more shells. "Besides, I still got three guests hauled up in that there inn, so I ain't goin' nowhere!"

Jubee ducked right as two Iroko Minions butt slammed the top of the barrel down on top of him. A second later, a narrow wooden slat opened on the side of the barrel, and the end of a shotgun poked out. The Barrakewdo shop owner was shockingly prepared for a combat scenario.

"Hurry up and get savin' my inn, missy, or yer gonna find yerself outta a job!" Jubee's muffled voice shouted as he turned to blast another group of the mischievous wooden creatures.

"Save the Inn? With these two numbskulls? Right. What do we... where... HOW?!" Nora stammered as she calculated whether it was even possible.

"Right!" She stabbed a finger at them abruptly. "Who remembers Master Yobei's sixteen steps to battlefield engagement?"

They turned towards each other, hoping that the other would have an answer. They shrugged.

"Really?! Neither of you?" Nora closed her eyes and blew out a shaky, nervous breath. "That figures. Alright. Step one..."

But Raz interrupted her with a groan.

"Come oooooon, who needs all that Master mumbo jumbo? Let's just get out there kick their butts already!"

"STEP ONE," Nora said again, refusing to be rushed, "Assess the enemy to understand your offensive strategy better. Master Kozomo told us that Iroko Minions are part of the Storm Shadows originating from the World Tree. They were first recorded by a Zeeks the traveler in the Chronicles of —"

She flinched as the wood of the table exploded outwards from an impact on the other side. Ten feet away, several Iroko Minions took turns picking each other up and bowling themselves at their improvised cover. The fat Iroko Minion, whose body had just cracked their table ran back, arms raised in victory, as the others rejoiced. The chaotic destruction was merely a game to them.

"Nora, we don't have time for a history lesson right now. Just boil it down to the key points!" Raz said between gritted teeth.

"Key points?! How are you supposed to come up with a plan of action if you don't know all the facts?" Nora whined.

The Iroko Minions called out enthusiastically as the fat one rolled at the table again. Raz quickly leaned over the table, scooped up the rolling Iroko in both hands before it impacted, then turned and punted it into the ocean.

"Ayeeeeeeeeeeee!" it squealed as it sailed away into the horizon.

"KEY POINTS, NORA! KEY POINTS!" Raz cried again.

"I'm trying! It's hard to think when you're interrupting me all the time!" Nora complained.

"Uhhhhhh guys? My leg feels kinda funny..." Rin squeaked.

They both turned and saw Rin wobble and fall flat on his face. One of the vines had wrapped itself around his leg. The Iroko Minions hummed. The vine constricted and pulled the big Moonken up and away from them. Raz lunged to catch his wrist, but he missed and ate sand. Before they knew it, Rin was dangling above the beach upside down from one leg like a fish caught on a hook. He thrashed around as several Iroko Minions pointed, laughing hysterically.

"I can't feel my leg!" Rin called out more as a statement of fact than in panic.

Nora coughed. Her eyes darted back and forth as if reading a page of information in her mind. "Um. Key point number one. See those vines? Those thorns are filled with poison that causes paralysis, so…"

"That might have been useful to know five minutes ago!" Raz exclaimed, pointing to Rin.

"I was getting to it," Nora said, shifting uncomfortably. "And don't blame me! I TOLD you that doing this on our own was a bad idea!"

"Augh! Do you ALWAYS have to be such a—"

THUNK!

The tip of a boning knife drove itself through the table between the two Moonken. Raz glanced over the edge and saw a group of Iroko Minions rolling with laughter as they rummaged through the kitchen supplies. He ducked down just in time to avoid a spatula flying towards him.

"Guys, any other time I'd be more than happy to let you scream at each other, but could you please, GIVE IT A REST, ALREADY?!" Rin called out as he bobbed around helplessly. Raz and Nora looked at each other and nodded.

"He's right. Arguing isn't going to help," Raz said, as he swatted away another Iroko Minion, "Even though I was totally right."

"Raz!" Rin shrieked.

"Right, sorry, sorry…" He gestured to Rin. "Can't you cut him down or something? We're sitting ducks out here!" Nora took a brief glance and shook her head.

"No can do, the sand under him is all vines now. If I did, he'd be plant food," she replied. From the far end of the beach, Jubee's shotgun blasted a group of Irokos that were trying to flank them. Raz's eyes darted his eyes between Rin, Jubee, and the door of the inn. He shouldered Klu's massive carrot.

"Alright, new plan! You protect Rin and Jubee while I go in the inn, kick some Iroko butt and save those people!" Raz declared.

"That's it?!" Nora cried. "That's a TERRIBLE plan!"

"COVER ME!" Raz shouted as he rose to his feet.

"Wait!"

But it was too late. Raz had already begun running across the open beach towards the inn, screaming at the top of his lungs. He held the carrot lowered in front of him like a battering ram. "Come on carrot! DO something!"

The Iroko Minions converged on him, drawn to the activity like children to a new plaything.

A mixed volley of homemade ninja stars from above and shotgun blasts from across the beach sent little wooden bodies flying in every direction as Raz charged and gained momentum. He was close, just a few more seconds.

"Raz, look out!" Rin warned as Raz passed underneath him. A group of ten Iroko Minions formed a line in front of him, hands clasped together. They all jumped as one, forming a tripwire with their bodies. It was too late to slow down. Raz heard a loud, deep whoosh of air then saw Nora's huge boomerang slam into all ten of them with exacting precision.

"Go go go!" she called out behind him.

"GUUUUUNGA LAAAGUUUUUNGA!" Raz screamed as he slammed the carrot into the door. The wooden planks splintered off of their hinges and sailed across the room on impact.

Not bad!

Raz looked down at the vegetable in wonderment. Maybe Klu wasn't crazy after all.

To his left was an Iroko Minion staring back at him from the front desk of Jubee's Rock House. It had fixed a small wispy twig on its face in the semblance of a mustach, and a broken piece of glass over its eye, resembled a monocle. It politely squeaked and gestured as if it were ready to check Raz in for a relaxing evening. It rang the bell a few times and giggled incessantly.

Raz responded by punching it into the wall. They might have looked sweet, but turn your back for one second and that's when they get you. He turned as the Irokos all hummed in unison once more. Outside, Nora cupped her hands over her mouth to shout at him.

"Raz, hurry up and get outta—" the rest was cut off. She disappeared from view, as a swarm of vines took over the entrance of the Inn and slithered a few feet towards the front desk before halting. In the distance, he could hear the muffled cracks of Jubee's shotgun and the wooden thwacks of Nora's boomerang as the battle on the beach raged on.

With the leaves of the carrot gripped tightly in his hand, he ascended the stairs, banging his fist against the walls and shouting at the top of his lungs. At the top of the stairs, a tanned man and a blonde-haired woman in their pajamas poked their heads out of a doorway to see what all the commotion was about.

"Hey! You!" Raz exclaimed and pointed the carrot at them. "Get your pants on and follow me! We're getting out of here!"

"See, honey? I told you someone would come for us!" the man proclaimed. The woman looked Raz up and down and grimaced.

"A Moonken?" she asked, hands on her hips. She didn't sound pleased.

"Now, now, honey," the man said behind a forced smile, "there's no need to be rude, what with all the killer plants outside…"

"Yeah, yeah, you can thank me later, we don't have much time," Raz said. He'd heard it all before. "Where's the kid?"

Raz scanned the hallway. "GAH!" He yelped, nearly jumping out of his skin as a tiny hand tugged at his robe from behind. At first, he thought his opponents had snuck up on him. But he saw the familiar face of the boy from the window earlier. He hid behind Raz's legs, seemingly just as scared of the other couple as he was of Irokos.

"Hey, that was easy! Come on, we can go out the back," he said and turned back to the stairs.

Outside, the Irokos hummed again, louder than before. At the bottom of the stairs, Raz saw the vines slithering up the first step. It wouldn't be long before the first floor was covered in vines and swarming with the little wooden bastards.

"Oooookay then, change of plans! You two," Raz pointed at the couple, "start collecting sheets! We're gonna have to climb out!"

"Huh? Sheets? That's it?" the man squeaked.

"Unless you're planning to jump two stories down to the walkway?" Raz suggested.

"Well... no. But you're a Moonken, right? Can't you fight your way out or use your weird Moonken powers or whatever?" the man mumbled.

Raz sighed. Some things never changed. "Moonken powers, eh? Sorry pal, but my giant gryphon wings and laser eyes only come out on a full moon," Raz replied sarcastically. The man's face went red and his eyes darted with embarrassment to the floor. Raz was about to say something much nastier, but he caught the kid looking up at him and decided against it.

"Just get the sheets and be snappy about it," Raz ordered. "And if you see any of those little wooden guys, don't mess with 'em, they're nastier than they look. Oh! And whatever you do, don't touch those vines," Raz added. If the vine's poison had affected Rin that quickly, he could only imagine what it could do to a normal human.

Muffled gunshots and shouts could be heard outside on the beach where Nora, Rin, and Jubee were still fighting.

Raz moved into the first room on his right, toward the
window that overlooked the front of the inn. The kid
trailed behind him.

"Where do you think you're going?!" the woman
called out.

"I'm gonna buy us some time!" Raz called back and
threw open the window, carefully avoiding any stray vines
as he poked his head out to assess the situation.

Down below, Nora danced between the encroaching
vines and swung her boomerang to keep the Iroko Minions
at bay, while Jubee continued blasting away with his
shotgun. Almost at eye level with Raz, but upside down,
was Rin, still hanging from his foot.

"How's it going out here, Rin?" he asked.

"I can't feel my butt!" Rin reported in a matter-of-fact
tone as he threw homemade ninja stars down at the Irokos
below him. The leg that wasn't entangled in the vine hung
limply at his side. The paralysis was spreading fast. Raz
flinched as two Irokos bounced off the wall right beside the
window. Nora brought the boomerang out in front of her
like a shield and glared up at Raz.

"Raz! Hurry up! If my hunch is right, something
worse is gonna show up real soon!"

"I'm working on it!" Raz shouted in reply. "The first
floor's overrun! We've gotta go out the back! Can you keep
'em off the walkway?"

Something worse? He was about to ask what she meant
but before he had the chance, she leaned back to dodge a
broom handle careening toward her face.

"We'll try, kid!" Jubee called out from the slat in the
barrel. "But I'm runnin' low on ammo out here!"

The situation was deteriorating fast. The vines
had spread even further, only a third of the beach was
untouched by the poisonous vines now. Raz leaned out and
gave Rin a reassuring pat on the back.

"I'm counting on you, Rin!" he said.

"Leave it to me!" Rin replied and pulled a flash bomb out of his bag.

From the hallway, someone screamed. Raz darted out of the room and saw two Iroko Minions slowly advancing on the couple who were pinned at the other end of the hall. The Iroko Minions swung pieces of the poisonous vines above their head like whips.

"Hey! Over here, you ugly little bowling balls!" Raz called out. The two Iroko Minions turned and ran towards him. He dodged backward, narrowly avoiding the whip-like vines. The kid clung nervously to Raz's leg as they advanced.

Damn it! He swore to himself. *If only I had something a little...*

He turned his head and saw the mud-caked root of the massive carrot, still in his hand.

...bigger.

The two Irokos jumped back in surprise as Raz swung the massive carrot down in front of him. One was too slow and took the full force of the swing, smashing clean through the wall. The other charged and swung the vine at Raz's face.

Without thinking, Raz held the carrot upright like a shield and moved himself and the kid behind it. The vine hit the carrot and got stuck.

"Neee heeee?" The Iroko Minion squeaked with uncertainty. Then Raz kicked it through the ceiling.

"Whoa!" The boy cheered, kicking and punching the air enthusiastically. The couple blinked as if they were having a hard time believing what they'd just seen. From below, Raz heard the hollow footfalls of dozens of Iroko Minions filing into the lobby.

"Time to go!" Raz called and ran towards the other end of the hallway. He corralled the three humans into the last room. Raz kicked open the window, the same one he'd seen the boy's face in before. He stuck his head out and heard the sounds of fighting from the beach but couldn't make out where his friends were from there.

"You guys okay over there?!" he called out.

"Oh, hey Raz! My left arm stopped working!" Rin called back with strange enthusiasm.

"Hurry it up, Raz! More of them are showing up!" Nora cried.

"There's nothing to tie these sheets off to in here!" the man cried behind him. Raz looked around and saw he was right. Jubee had converted the room into storage. The sound of wooden feet were getting closer.

"I've got an idea," Raz said and snatched the sheets out of his hands. He started to tie the sheets around the carrot.

"Are you crazy?" the human girl cried out.

"No! Jeez. Why does everyone keep saying that?" Raz replied and ran into the hallway. He turned the carrot sideways and braced it against the doorframe as the couple looked at him with uncertainty. "Don't worry, this is no ordinary carrot!"

A group of Irokos charged up the stairs across from him. In their hands they wielded regular-sized carrots like swords. Apparently, he had given them some ideas. He punched and kicked at them as they charged, but it felt like for every one he hit two more took its place.

"Go! I can't fend them off forever!" Raz shouted.

The couple clawed at each other to go down the rope first. The man leapt ahead, while the girl cussed him out bitterly. About ten seconds later, the girl went down next, much more slowly.

Come on, come on…hurry up!

Only the boy remained. He looked worried. Raz forced a smile.

"Go! I'll be fine!"

The boy climbed onto the sheets and started to descend. The wooden beasts converged into a swarm in the hallway,

All Raz could do was thrash his limbs wildly and hope he hit something.

He cried out as a sharp stinging pain erupted from his left shoulder. He looked down and saw the thorn of a poisonous vine sticking out of his flesh.

"GRRRRRRRAH!" he cried and threw out a huge sweeping kick to give himself some space. The sheets went slack, as the carrot dropped to the floor. That meant the boy had made it down safely.

Time to go!

He snatched his weapon and ran at the window full tilt, jumping through the small opening head first. He landed with a crash at the wooden walkway. He raised himself up just in time to see the boy and the couple running under the sign and towards the forest. So much for gratitude, but at least they were safe.

He winced at the pain from the wound in his left shoulder. The poison was already taking effect, his left arm tingled and began to go limp.

The Iroko Minions all started chanting in unison. Each time they hummed and chanted it was more deliberate and structured than the last. Above him, he saw the vines wrap themselves around the back of the inn, growing faster than he thought was possible.

Something had changed.

Raz scrambled to his feet and ran back down the staircase to where Nora, Rin, and Jubee were still locked in combat. His jaw dropped.

The beach as he'd seen it from the window minutes earlier was no more. The vines had taken all but a small sliver of sand near the walkway. From the far end of the beach where Jubee's barrel was, a curved canopy of vines had formed and nearly blotted out the sun. Nora whirled and batted off groups of Iroko Minions on the small patch of sand that was left.

"You better tell me those people got out, Raz!" Nora shouted to him as he came up next to her.

"They're safe!" he reported back.

"Really? You actually pulled it off?" she didn't even try to hide the surprise in her voice.

Raz patted his carrot and moved up beside her. "Turns out Klu's secret weapon is the real deal," he said. "How's it going out here?"

"Peachy! What's it look like?!" she shot back. He raised up his carrot and stood next to her, side by side.

"What's with these things? They should be giving up by now," Raz reasoned. The last time he'd fought Iroko Minions they'd run back into the forest after taking a few hits. These ones were different - more coordinated - more deadly. Something was seriously wrong.

"That's what I was trying to tell you. Master Kozomo says when this many Iroko Minions are in one place it can only mean one thing..."

She cocked her head to the side like she'd heard something and shoved Raz backwards with both hands just in time as two vines shot out and wrapped around each of her legs.

"Ahhhhh, crap!" was all she managed to shout before being pulled into the air.

Then, all at once, everything went quiet.

The Iroko Minions, every last one of them, stopped in their tracks, stopped their playful destruction. They all turned, as if on cue, and calmly arranged themselves in neat rows around the edge of the vines.

About fifteen feet behind Jubee, a small figure emerged, no larger than a child. It was wire thin and draped in an ornate woven cloth. Wild, scraggly patches of weeds and underbrush jutted out from the back of a long beak-like wooden mask. Its eyes glowed white like slivers

of moonlight on a cold night. It strode forward, past Jubee's barrel and looked up towards the dangling figures of Rin and Nora.

Nora threw her boomerang at the creature but the throw went wide. Odd for Nora. It thudded into the sand near Raz's feet.

The creature narrowed its eyes up at her and waved a short gnarled staff. The vines instantly obeyed his command and wound around the two trapped Moonken like cocoons, covering them up to their shoulders. He waved the staff once more and Rin and Nora were flung into the wall of the inn, stuck there like flies in a spider web.

Raz stood shakily on the tiny patch of sand. He raised the carrot in front of him, not exactly sure what he intended to do with it. The creature laughed and all of the Iroko Minions joined in the mockery in perfect unison. The chaos had subsided, and they now moved and obeyed their master in perfect harmony.

An Irokomancer. It was controlling them, driving them forward. That's what Nora was trying to warn me about. Raz had heard stories as a kid, but they were rarely seen anymore.

"Foolish Moonken with their foolish weapons…" the Irokomancer hissed. Raz rolled out his shoulders, the left one where he'd been hit was now entirely numb. He swung the carrot down in front of him.

"Hey, twig face! This here's a weapon of the Masters! Show it the proper respect!" Raz taunted.

The Irokomancer turned towards him. Turned away from where Jubee was hiding.

Big mistake, plant-for-brains.

Suddenly, Jubee burst out of the top of the barrel, shotgun drawn and leveled at the Irokomancer's head.

"How's this fer a foolish weapon?!" Jubee cried. The Irokomancer's eyes went wide with surprise and fear. *Got him.* The Barrakewdo smirked and pulled the trigger.

Click.

Click. Click.

The smile disappeared from Jubee's face. "Ahhh fishsticks," he grunted in disappointment then dove back inside the barrel just as the vines wrapped themselves around it like a snake. The proprietor of the inn belted out a string of expletives as the barrel was thrown out of the way.

The Irokomancer turned towards Raz, as did the hundreds of Iroko Minions under its control. Jubee was trapped and out of ammo. Rin and Nora were very literally tangled up. This far out from Crescent Isle, there would be no rescue from Master Klu, no one to swoop in and save the day this time.

Their fate would be determined by a single Moonken with an oversized carrot.

CHAPTER 12
THE SECRETS OF KUNG FULIO

Raziel Tenza faced a tunnel of menacing vines. The light from the sun fought its way through the cracks in the canopy and cast strange oblong shadows on what was once the beach in front of Jubee's Rock House. In front of him, stood one frail, small and yet incredibly powerful Irokomancer. With the flick of its wrist, its movements were mirrored throughout the length of the tendrils. The Iroko Minions, no longer a bumbling, chaotic swarm of butt-slapping, stick-poking and nose-flicking wooden pranksters, now hummed and sang in unison, aligning themselves in a perfect circle around their master. Slaves to his will.

Raz saw this as his advantage. The Irokomancer was the brain - take him out and everything he controlled would go down with it.

No big deal. How hard could it be? This wasn't some

scaly evil beast like Doken - it was a twig. And now he had the carrot. The vegetable alone had already practically transformed him into a one-man fighting machine - in his mind anyway. One solid hit was all it would take. Admittedly, that would be a little easier if the ground between them weren't completely covered in deadly paralyzing thorns. But it seemed that the Irokomancer couldn't stretch the floor of vines out any farther. So at least he had that going for him.

The Irokomancer paced back and forth from a safe distance, sizing up its foe. As it moved, its hands flared out, spiraling the spindly fingers as if he were casting a spell on his minions.

"Moonken... Artifact..." the Irokomancer hissed. "Where is... the artifact?" As it spoke, its words echoed in hundreds of whispers through the mouths of the Iroko Minions.

Raz looked around what was visible of Jubee's general store. "Yeah, I think you got the wrong address, pal! The only Moonken artifact around here is Nora's sense of humor!"

The moment he said it, he felt that he would have slapped his own forehead if his hand wasn't paralyzed. His quips always sounded better in his head.

"Muuuuuuubffft!" Rin tried desperately to chime in, but the paralysis agent had rendered his lips all but useless. However, that did nothing to discourage him, and he soldiered on as if he was talking entirely normally.

"Cmmm ooooohhl! Ooo gaaah diiiis!" Rin managed to wail before his tongue flopped out of his mouth and hung there like a tired dog. A line of drool slowly dripped in front of his numb face.

"Rin is right!" Nora agreed, sticking her chin up to keep her face as far away as possible from the cocoon of vines around her.

"Wha? You understood that?" Raz squeaked, his eyes peeled on the Irokomancer.

"He said, 'you've got this!' And he's right! I... uh... I believe in you?" she said with uncertainty. Raz took his eyes off of his foe for a moment to glance at her. All that poison must have gone to her brain.

"You really think so?" Raz raised an eyebrow.

She coughed. "Well, maybe I wouldn't go that far. But if you screw up, we're pretty much goners! SO DON'T SCREW UP!" she clarified with an understandable hint of anxiety in her voice.

How reassuring.

The Irokomancer was infuriatingly patient. The poison from Raz's wound had already made the fingers in his left hand numb. If he was going to put a stop to this, he needed to do it fast.

"Come on, twiggy, I don't have all day here!" Raz shouted. But the wooden wizard-creature continued to pace far out of his range.

"What? Don't want to fight me, mano-a-mano?" Raz shouted impatiently. "Fine, have it your way!"

Raz threw the carrot down in front of him and reached over to grab Nora's boomerang, still stuck in the sand near his feet. It was surprisingly heavy in his hands. He grunted, wound back his arm and lobbed it with all of his body weight.

It wasn't as graceful as one of Nora's throws, but it did the job. The creature flinched and threw up its arms feebly as the boomerang rocketed towards it. In response, a wave of Iroko Minions threw themselves in front of the oncoming projectile, clutching to each other to form a living wall. The shell of Minions hardened as the boomerang bounced off and disappeared into the tangle of vines.

Not one to let a single failure stop him, Raz tried again, kicking a stray bucket at the Irokomancer. It led to the same result - another wave of Irokos took the hit before it reached their master.

Raz cursed under his breath. That was an annoying trick. He could throw stuff at him all day and he'd never run out of minions. At least not before Raz was reduced to a paralyzed, gibbering mess.

"Raz, you're a genius!" Nora exclaimed.

"I am? But he keeps blocking me!" Raz yelled back.

"Correction," she said, unable to resist the urge to lecture him, even in the face of imminent doom, "The Iroko Minions blocked you! He's got no technique! He was wide open back there!"

"He was?" Raz asked as he picked up his carrot and placed it in front of him defensively.

"Duh! Don't you notice anything that's going on around you? All you gotta do is get around his guard and he's done for!" Nora said, like it was the simplest thing in the

world. Still, he realized her quick assessment was right. The Irokomancer had lots of tricks, but martial prowess wasn't one of them. It was getting up close to him that would be the tricky part.

The Irokomancer didn't like the display of team spirit and flicked a spindly finger in Nora's direction. The vines that held her wriggled to life.

"Raz! I REALLY DO believe in y—" Her cry was cut off as the vines curled around her mouth leaving nothing visible but her eyes.

For a second there, it almost sounded like she was about to say she believed in him. For real this time. She'd never gotten behind him like that before. It was almost enough to give him the feels.

"Enough games, Moonken scum," the Irokomancer growled and raised its hands into the air.

Four vines rose up from the ground in front of Raz and loomed over him. He could guess what was coming next.

It was time to move. Lining the front of Jubee's Rock House and leading all the way back along the length of the beach were a series of metal lamp posts. Through some miracle, the posts hadn't been overgrown. It was as if the vines had difficulty taking hold on the cold metal.

The Irokomancer brought down its hands, and as it did the vines crashed down towards Raz like the fingers of a giant hand swatting a fly.

His left arm was now numb. He took up the carrot in his right and leaped into the air, kicking off the vines' stiff bark as they rocketed past him. The top of the lamppost rose up to meet him, as he landed hard, he wobbled frantically to maintain his balance. He glanced over towards Nora and could practically hear her screaming telepathically to bend his knees and straighten up like she always did after Dou's meditations.

So that's what he did. He absorbed the movement of the

swaying post and regained his balance. It turned out, Nora was right about that all along - maybe he'd thank her when this was all over. But probably not.

The Irokomancer threw out its arms and the vines launched toward him once more. They instantly exploded into a shower of splinters as Raz's carrot blasted through them. The weight of the vegetable dragged him around in circles, until he finally spun to a slow stop.

"Hah! Your stupid vines are no match for the secrets of Kung Fulio! Come on, plant-for-brains, I could stay up here all da— OH CRA—" He panicked as his foot nearly slipped off the post. The paralysis had spread down to his leg.

The Irokomancer narrowed its glowing eyes and raised an open palm above its head.

"Let us put that to the test," it snarled as three Iroko

Minions placed a pile of footlong razor-sharp purple thorns into its waiting hand. With a flick of the wrist, it hurled the spear-like thorn towards Raz. With only one arm that still worked, he barely raised the carrot up in time to block it. The thorn stuck into the skin of the carrot. Poison oozed from the tip. The puppet-master creature flung out a barrage of thorns in a rapid-fire. The Moonken struggled to maintain his balance and narrowly blocked the onslaught. Before long, almost a dozen purple spines were sticking out of the carrot.

Raz knew that he only had moments before his secret weapon was reduced to a pulp. The thorns stopped flying and the humming began once more. Below him, dozens of Iroko Minions peeled off from the leading group and began to shake at the lamp post violently. Raz teetered atop the metal post, as more thorns began to thud against his defensive carrot once more.

Raz leaped to the next lamp post. Mid-flight, he kicked an Iroko Minion that tried to tackle him towards its master, and once more, he saw a wave of minions leap up to block the blow. The Irokomancer was getting cocky. It wasn't changing tactics. Nora was right - he had no technique.

Landing on the next post was a little harder. He

could barely put any weight on his left leg as the paralysis continued to spread down his body.

It took everything he had to keep his weight on his good leg while keeping the carrot gripped firmly over his shoulder. At that moment, an Iroko Minion launched itself at him from above. It was too late to block it.

But to his surprise, nothing happened. He looked down to find that the Iroko Minion had impaled itself on one of the purple thorns that had been stuck in the side of his carrot.

Hmmm...that's interesting. Sometimes your best plan is to improvise. Raz thought to himself.

His strength was failing. The paralysis had spread throughout most of his body. He had an idea, but to do it, he was going to need more of those thorns - a lot more.

"Hey! Twiggy! You missed!" Raz taunted and let his now-numb left arm flop in the air for his opponent to see. "Look! You can't even hit a one-armed Moonken!"

The Irokomancer fumed in frustration and held out both hands to its side as a stream of Iroko Minions ran up with more purple thorns.

It had taken the bait.

Nora and Rin, still paralyzed wrapped in vines up to their eyeballs, stared helplessly in horror at the unfolding situation.

Raz turned to them and winked with a cocky nod that displayed an absurd level of confidence. Judging by the looks in their eyes, it didn't do much to reassure them.

The Irokomancer started throwing the sharp purple thorns in a torrent with both hands. Raz didn't need to block them all,

but he needed to get as many as he could embed into the carrot to

make the next part work. A few of the thorns grazed his cheek, his upper thigh, but he didn't care. It was a slow poison. If this didn't work he was done for anyway.

The Irokomancer cried out in rage, unleashing a dense wave of new thorns. He made a snapping sound with his clawed fingers as he screamed a mesmerizing cry. The Iroko Minions surrounding him formed a wave that barreled towards Raz, echoing their masters war cry.

At the last possible second, Raz leapt over the wave of Iroko Minions, sending them crashing into the post with such force that it sent boulders and other debris flying off the side of the Rock House into the forest.

He managed an impressive one-footed landing on the final light post at the far end of the beach closest to Jubee's hut. Closest to the Irokomancer. He looked down at his carrot. It was now so full of the poisonous thorns that it resembled an orange and purple hedgehog. He knew he couldn't take another hit.

It was now or never.

With half of his body numb, he raised the carrot above his head, and launched himself across the sea of thorns towards the Irokomancer. Right on cue, the creature threw up its hands, and a hardened wall of Iroko Minions formed in front of him to stop the blow.

Just as Raz thought he would.

He swung the thorn-covered carrot at the wall. But the carrot didn't bounce off like everything else had before. It stuck firmly INTO the wood, giving him enough of a foothold to launch off of it like a diving board. Raz flew up and over the defensive wall.

The Irokomancer's eyes went wide as it stood there, realizing it's fatal error. Its body remained stunned as the Moonken plunged downwards, fist raised in front of him.

This would be his only chance.

Raz's fist collided into the creature's mask with incredible force. But the momentum of the jump sent his body hurling past the creature. His body flew directly into the floor of paralyzing vines. He felt the sting of his face slamming into the dirt, and then quickly stopped feeling anything at all. The hundreds of thorns covered his body, slowing him to complete immobile and helpless paralysis. His neck rested to one side, leaving him gazing back towards the Irokomancer, Jubee's Rock House and his imprisoned friends.

The puppet-master's body stood motionless as well. Its cloak flapped in the wind. Until slowly, it turned, taking a faltering step backward, and stumbling. Its menacing eyes narrowed at Raz as if it were ready to attack again.

Then, a crack formed. Small at first, it spread down the entire length of the Irokomancer's mask. An explosion of wind rushed outwards as the Irokomancer screamed in anguish, twisting its limbs towards the sky. It jerked its limbs awkwardly as its body gradually stiffened then froze and went brittle.

All around Raz, the vines began to recede and shrivel up, dissolving into nothing. The canopy above shrunk away, leaving a peaceful blue sky. Without their master, the Iroko Minions gripped their heads in a dizzy rush, and fell face-first into the dirt where they stood. They withered away like dead leaves. It was as if an entire season had passed in an instant. The cocoons of vines that held Nora and Rin dried and peeled off the wall, and the two Moonken fell limp onto the sand of the beach.

Raz saw what remained of his carrot fall upright into the sand then crack in half, finally giving out from all the abuse. But that didn't matter, it had done just what Klu had promised. Raz had unleashed a hidden potential he never even knew he had.

Though he couldn't move his neck anymore, he heard the top of Jubee's barrel pop open as the Barrakewdo emerged once more.

"You did it lil' feller!" Jubee cried out in celebration.

In front of Raz, the Irokomancer's body withered. Now nothing more than a lifeless statue, it stood frozen in an eternal hateful stare. Abruptly, the thin, wispy shape of its body cracked and blew away in a cloud of dust.

The cracked wooden mask fell to the ground. It was all that remained.

Raziel Tenza had done it.

CHAPTER 13

LEVELING UP BEFORE DOWN

R az found himself engulfed in utter darkness. Not the reassuring blackness of sleep or the quiet blackness of night. No, this blackness had more of a mahogany smell, mixed with the scent of seawater and sweat.

Like a sack of 'taters, Jubee flipped Raz's limp body over to face the sunlight, clapping his fishy hands together as if he'd just completed a hard day's work.

"Alright l'il whipper snapper. There ya go!" He said and clapped Raz on the shoulder. "Got y'all in one place now! Now, where'd I put that dern anti-paralysis potion?"

He'd lined up the three limp-bodied, paralyzed Moonken side by side in front of the inn unceremoniously like three rolled-up tents. Jubee's storefront was a mess, not totally destroyed, but a mess nonetheless. He put his fins on his hips and surveyed it all with an expression that leaned more towards irritation than sadness. "Good gravy Marie. This here's gonna take a while to get right again."

"Hrrrrrrrr eeeeeeeee aaaaaaaaaahhh!" Nora gurgled from her paralyzed throat. Even drowned in spittle, Nora still managed to convey an air of mild annoyance. Agreeing wholeheartedly, Rin blew air out of his paralyzed mouth in a stream of spit bubbles.

"I'm workin' on it, I'm workin' on it!" Jubee called back as he rummaged through the remains of his shop. "Y'all should count yerselves lucky. If y'all weren't Moonken that poison'd probably woulda killed ya by now."

From where Raz was placed, he had a perfect view of the prim and proper Nora flopping around and slobbering like the rest of them. If he could smile, he certainly would have done so at that moment. However, on account of the massive quantities of paralyzing poison coursing through his veins, his lips only jerked and twitched into a snarl while his right eyelid broke into a fit of spasms. Given that Nora was still alive and not being digested by Storm Shadows, Raz figured that little miss goody-two-shoes would have a few apologies to make, perhaps? Maybe she'd back off on all the lecturing for a week or two. Or forever.

One could only hope.

Beyond amusement, Raz was also overwhelmingly proud of himself. There's no way he was going to be the laughing stock of Crescent Isle. Not anymore. He'd defeated an Irokomancer. He'd saved Jubee's Rock house - by himself.

With nothing but a carrot.

This was the stuff that legends were made of!

"Ah! Here we go!" Jubee exclaimed. He pulled out a jar of blue liquid from under a pile of sand, brushed it off, and carried it over to the three Moonken. "One anti-paralysis potion, comin' up!"

Jubee dumped the potion over their bodies

haphazardly. The healing effect was almost instantaneous. All three Moonken squirmed in discomfort as pins and needles spread from their chests to their fingertips. After a time, they leaned up and started to shake and test their limbs..

Raz turned towards Rin and smiled. He couldn't help it.

"Thabt…" Rin started then spat a few times and slapped his face to reset the muscles necessary for speech. "Raz, that was incred—"

"… incredibly stupid." Nora finished for him. In an instant, Raz's smile vanished. She brushed herself off, noting with horror all of the rips and tears in her robes. Raz sat, slack-jawed with disbelief. He must have heard her wrong.

"Uhhh… hold on, let's back up just a bit," Raz offered. "Want to try that again? I think you meant to say 'incredibly brave' or 'incredibly badass'? In case you didn't notice, I just took out that Irokomancer chump and saved your hiney."

Nora sighed and picked up her boomerang, inspecting it for damage. "Oh! My hero," she said sarcastically as she batted her eyes at him. "Yes you did," then she gestured at the mess around them, "and in only MOST recklessly and irresponsibly way possible!"

Raz squeezed the bridge of his nose and closed his eyes,

Jubee

hoping that when he opened them the Nora in front of him would be replaced by the new, appreciative Nora that had taken shape in his mind in the last half hour or so.

"Irresponsible? Reckless? What are you talking about?" he demanded.

"Ugh, you can't be serious! How about that moronic idea of yours to get hundreds of poisonous thorns thrown at you?"

"Uh... Yeah! That was the GENIUS of MY plan! Thanks to that I was able to get around his defense!" Raz puffed out his chest and looked away proudly.

Nora scoffed and pointed to the spot on the wall where she and Rin were plastered not long before.

"WE WERE RIGHT BEHIND YOU! If you'd missed or he'd thrown wide, Rin and I would have been ripped to shreds instead of that stupid carrot!"

"But I did block them! And... and..." he stammered, "Leave my carrot out of this!" he yelled back, and then trailed off in a mumble, "it's not stupid."

"And don't even get me STARTED about that final jump of yours!" she continued, undeterred. It seemed the lectures were far from over.

"What? YOU were the one who told me to get in close, remember?" Raz said, not believing his ears.

"You put your life in danger for the sake of one hit! ONE HIT!" she screamed again, incredulously.

"So? What's your point?" Raz wondered, completely baffled how anyone could see that leap, that stupendous orchestration of Moonken, carrot, and punch, as anything but amazing and heroic.

"What if you missed?!" she countered, her voice echoing against the rocks and going out to sea.

Raz simply cocked his neck and stared at her with a baffled look on his face. There was no point in trying to argue with Nora when she got this way, so he didn't bother.

"I'll tell you what would have happened," she blared, "You would have died, right along with the rest of us!"

Raz rose to his feet, he couldn't take this sitting down. Literally.

"I didn't have a choice!" he screamed back at her. "It was the only way to save you guys!"

Nora swallowed and darted her eyes away.

"I'm not saying you weren't brave Raz, I'm saying you should have thought things through for once. The Masters say that action without thought is like jumping into an angry sea with a blindfold."

Raz groaned and rolled his eyes as he disregarded her comment. "Stop it with the riddles and puzzles already! Jeez. Just say what you mean straight up for once!"

"It means," she growled, "that you got lucky this time. But if you keep acting impulsively, that reckless hero act of yours will backfire on you one of these days."

Rin coughed and tried to edge himself in between Raz and Nora before things got out of hand.

"But Nora, you have to admit, Raz… well… he kinda NAILED it. It's like Shadowmaster Kito says, sometimes the best plan is to improvise!" he chimed in, enthusiastic to add his own knowledge of ninjitsu to the discussion.

"See?! Rin gets it!" Raz nodded aggressively, grateful to have backup.

"Ninja Arts," Nora poked Rin so hard that he stumbled back, "are forbidden in the monastery! Rin!" The hint of venom in her voice was unmissable. She'd never accepted his obsession with the shadow arts.

Rin slumped back down onto the steps without a word. Raz felt the sting too. Only seconds after regaining the use of her mouth, Nora's words only reminded him why he didn't want to ask for her help in the first place.

It was clear that she would not be of any help to them after all. And it had nothing to do with what was right or wrong. It was because who he was. What' she'd already decided about him. "You know, what's your problem with me anyway?"

She recoiled in astonishment, surprised by his sudden change in tone.

"I don't have a probl-"

Raz quickly interrupted her by poking her in the center of her chest.

"So what if I don't plan twenty steps ahead or follow every stick in the mud rule about fighting? Sometimes you gotta take longshots to win. And just maaaayybe a longshot's exactly what you NEEDED in this situation! If I took your advice and did everything by the book, you and Rin would be fertilizer right about now. Call me crazy, but maybe I care too much about my friends to let that happen!" Raz shouted angrily.

"I didn't mean —" she paused, trying to find her footing once more, "I only meant that you guys need to take your training seriously or…"

"Nora…" Rin slid between them, and pushed hard to create a little breathing room. "Ya know maybe he's right. I mean, whether it was perfect form or by the book or whatever, he DID save our butts!"

"Well, I mean… I guess so," she admitted.

Rin turned to Raz and wrapped him up in a bear hug. "Thanks for saving our butts, pal! You might just make a great ninja yet!" Rin shuffled excitedly over to Nora and elbowed her in the ribs. She sighed and cleared her throat.

"Thanks… uh… Raz. I can't… uh… believe you, of all people —"

Rin elbowed her again, and she stopped.

"Thanks," she simplified.

Raz crossed his arms and grinned from ear to ear proudly. "You're welcome! See, that wasn't so hard!"

He huffed through his nose and marched over to the

bruised, cracked, mud-spattered carrot and picked it up delicately by the leaves. The top half almost immediately snapped away.

Nora cocked her eyebrow, not needing to put into words what was clearly on everyone's mind.

"What? I'm not letting this sweet baby out of my sight!" He lovingly patted it, causing another small chunk to break off. "Klu was right, this carrot was all I needed to unleash my inner badass!"

Jubee strolled over to them, tossing aside a broken piece of wood. "Y'all done recovered?"

"Thanks to you, Jubee!" Nora said, sweet as an angel. Raz glared at her. Lecturing and sarcastic remarks were apparently kept in reserve for her classmates.

"Good! I can't thank ya'll enough fer savin' my shop! Might even have to give you a raise, l'il missy!" he said and winked at Nora over his thick glasses. Raz puffed out his chest and was about to deliver a heroic, but humble, message when Nora beat him to the punch.

"Of course, Jubee. It's a Moonken's duty to help those in need," she said.

Who does she think she is? Raz thought with annoyance. The girl who wanted to run and get the Masters. Old fish face should have been thanking him, not her.

"And you two!" Jubee exclaimed and turned towards the Moonken boys, "I thought of somethin' REAL special to thank y'all!"

Raz and Rin eagerly held their hands out in from them, awaiting their reward. Decisively, Jubee slapped a piece of paper into each of their open palms. On the scrap of paper was a picture of a happy looking man with a beard and glasses giving a thumbs up. It was, Raz realized, likely what Jubee thought his disguise made him look like. Under the picture was a patch of blocky text:

"10% off all merchandise!" it read, and in smaller,

harder to read letters: "Certain restrictions apply. Not applicable on holidays or weekends."

Raz's hand fell to his side and he frowned so hard it squeezed his entire face into a tiny ball. "Ten percent?" he inquired, a hint of disappointment in his voice.

"Those're good fer life, ya know!" Jubee chirped.

"Raz! Don't be rude!" Nora scolded under her breath. "We're monks in training, not mercenaries. We don't need a reward!"

"I know that! I'm just saying, I only, ooooh, I don't know...DEFEATED AN IROKOMANCER SINGLE-HANDEDLY!" he yelled in Jubee's general direction.

Unimpressed, Nora glared at him coldly. "Gee, how could we forget? You've been SO humble about it," she said flatly.

The Barrakewdo contemplated this, calculating thousands of possible profit margins and deals in his mind.

"Hmmm, fine! Fifteen percent! But that's ma final offer, y' hear me? And restrictions still apply!" he called back.

Rin leaped victoriously into the air. "Daaaang! Fifteen percent? I wonder if he does magazine subscriptions...?"

"Hmph. For fifteen measly percent, you'd think I saved him from an invasion of raccoons," Raz sulked, kicking a broken chunk of a shelf into the ocean.

"Right, right. YOU saved him. Raz, our big hero, who saved Jubee's shop entirely on his own!" Nora interjected, with a healthy helping of sarcasm.

"Well," Raz said, dusting off his shoulders, "I DID do all the heavy lifting, when you really think about it."

Nora's eyes narrowed into slits as thin as a knife's edge. Her nostrils flared with wild indignity. "Why you egotistical, self-aggrandizing..."

"Heroes!" Rin cut her off, interjecting his own understanding of the situation. "We're all heroes here today."

"Heroes? How do you expla..." Nora scoffed.

"Because we beat the bad guys! We were the PERFECT team!" he declared in an odd, booming tone of voice.

"Huh?" Raz and Nora replied simultaneously.

Rin grabbed a nearby crate and turned it upside down. He hopped on top of it and straightening his back like a speaker on a podium. He cleared his throat.

"Friends, Moonken, fellow monks in training... Jubee," he said as an afterthought, to which Jubee nodded in acknowledgment and spat into a spittoon. "Today, three Moonken came together: Raz, Nora, and Rin," he gestured to each of them superfluously, "When that bird thing flew up to the window with a note, I could smell it in the air," he sniffed the air with a dramatic pause, "it was the smell... of DESTINY! And when those dastardly Storm Shadows showed up, it confirmed it!"

The formality of his speech began to wane somewhat, but what he lacked in pomp, he made up for in pizazz. "But did we back down? Did we give up? NO! We overcame! We persevered! We kicked ass! Today, Team NoRaRin... er... Team NoRiRaz...Nor..." he paused then gave up, "the ultimate fighting force was forged in the heat of combat!"

"HYEEEE HAW!" Jubee let out an excited whoop, flapping his fins together excitedly.

"And we're not gonna stop here!" Rin continued, "Because together we can achieve the impossible, climb the highest mountains, defeat the greatest enemies! And now that Raz and I have held up our end of the bargain, it's time for our unstoppable team to tackle their next mission: kick Nox and the Red Cobra's collective butts... right in the teeth! By that, I mean, we will, in fact, collect their butts, and kick them!" he exclaimed, then mumbled out of the side of his mouth, "Nevermind the last part about the teeth."

Raz applauded, and Jubee continued to slap his fins together next to his hut. In typical Nora fashion, she remained silent with her arms crossed in front of her.

"What d'ya say?" Rin asked, extending a hand to Nora. "Ready to help us take down the Cobras?"

Nora looked stern and did not respond for a long time, as she watched the waves roll in on the beach.

"No," she said simply.

With a crash, Rin tripped and fell off the podium before scrambling to his feet. With a single word, she'd dealt a crushing blow.

"W-Wait a second! What do you mean 'no'?!" he stammered.

"Yeah, what's the big idea? Whose side are you on, anyway?" Raz jumped to his friend's defense.

Nora started fixing her hair, as if abandoning her friends were the easiest thing in the world.

"Who said anything about sides? Stop and listen to yourselves. Nox isn't some demon or something. He's one of us!"

"Wait. WHAT? One of—" Raz cut himself off, unable to fathom the bold inaccuracy of such a statement. He stamped and paced like a pent up bull as Nora continued tying her hair up and fixing her uniform. Calmly. Cool as a cucumber.

"But you said you'd help us! You p-p-p-promised!" Rin pleaded as his lower lip quivered.

"What Rin is being too polite to say is, that we had a DEAL," Raz said, pointing his finger at Nora accusingly. "We helped you, just like we said we would. You owe us!"

"Yes, you helped me. But if you were the least bit observant, you'd notice that this is far from over," she replied casually. Raz was utterly baffled. He watched her as one would watch an alien creature.

"Not over?!" Raz parroted in disbelief. He looked at the empty beach, the remains of his glorious battle of Kung Fulio awakening. "I literally punched that Irokomancer so hard that he friggin' EXPLODED! It's done! We WON!"

Nora closed her eyes, took a deep breath then blew it out slowly, inviting the calm of the universe to flow through her.

"According to Master Kozomo, an Irokomancer hasn't been seen this close to Crescent Isle in over a hundred years," she explained and strolled over to where the Irokomancer's mask had fallen onto the floorboards of Jubee's hut. "This," she said, holding it up, "is the real reason we train as Moonken. Not to help a few innocent people, not to make ourselves feel better, not to be heroes, but to keep Speria in balance."

Raz's head was spinning. He didn't get it.

"What are you saying? Helping innocent people is the point. In every story about the Monks of Twilight, they defended the innocent people who couldn't defend themselves. Beating the bad guys and saving people was the whole point," Raz said.

"Look around you," she said calmly, "Do you think that all of this means victory?"

If this was some sort of test, Raz wasn't in the mood. It was time to draw a line in the sand and choose sides. If she wouldn't help them, then all of this was a waste of time. They were back to square one. He was proud of what he accomplished, and just like every other time back at the monastery, she wouldn't let him enjoy his victory. Not even for a second.

"It might not look pretty, but all of those

people are still alive. If that's not a victory, I don't know what is," Raz said, standing his ground. Nora didn't budge either, and Rin, still reeling from the dissolution of Team RinNoRaz, remained silent on the sidelines.

"That's exactly the kind of shortsighted answer that I expected from you, Raz," Nora said accusingly.

Raz stewed in anger. No matter what good he did, or how hard he tried it never seemed enough to live up to people's expectations of him.

"I suppose you think that if you beat Nox, then you'll be the big hero, right?" she posed the question casually, picking her boomerang up off the beach. "And just like that Irokomancer, you think that once Nox goes down all the bad stuff will go down with him... and we'll be the good guys," she continued, dusting the sand from the boomerang's surface.

"Of course!" Raz replied defensively. "Don't give me that 'Nox is one of us' crap. Just ask anyone whose life is miserable because of him. He might not be some Storm Shadows demon, but he's definitely one of the bad guys. And when we take him down, everybody wins. That's just about the purest form of winning that there is."

"If you believe that, then maybe you really are," Nora exhaled through her nose, deep in concentration, "the worst student at the monastery!"

Raz bit his lip, and his face turned red as he contained an internal scream. The frustration threatened to boil over inside of him. How could someone so book-smart, so wholly and utterly miss the point at a crucial moment like this?

"Don't you think that's a little harsh, Nora...?" Rin asked, trying his best to right the sinking ship of their alliance.

"It's not harsh, it's fair," Nora declared. "Your best buddy needs to get his head out of the clouds and realize that winning isn't going to solve all of his problems."

"What the heck is that supposed to mean?!" Raz demanded. "Since when does winning against the bad guys

NOT make you a winner?!"

"The Masters say that a single victory, not fully considered, leads to a hundred defeats," Nora recounted calmly. "Like I said, what happened here isn't over. The Masters need to know about this. Now. Your little problem with Nox and the Cobras will have to wait."

"Nox… Cobras… 'little problem'?!" Raz's words came out in concentrated, rage-filled bursts, the higher-functioning sides of his brain had almost completely shut off in a last-ditch effort to remain sane.

"Yes. Little problem," she said again, stinging Raz with indignation like a scorpion striking the heart. "We stumbled into something big here. I've got a feeling that Irokomancer was just the start."

"So you're just gonna leave us? Just like that?" Rin summarized glumly. Nora frowned as she turned to Rin and placed a hand on his shoulder.

"It's not that simple, Rin. I'll help you as soon as I can. Until then, just lay low and try to stay out of trouble," she said.

Cupping a hand over her eyes, she looked at the deep orange sky. She shot a withering look at Raz and swore under her breath, as if the passage of time itself were his fault. She marched over to Jubee.

"Jubee! I need to borrow one of your birds," she requested roughly.

Jubee's prized collection of loyal birds were known throughout the region to be among the Rock House owner's most prized possessions. That one of Jubee's fishy nature would choose to keep a whole collection of its own natural predators was considered eccentric by more than a few guests.

"Hmm? Which'n is it that you want?" Jubee asked, eyeing her suspiciously.

"Grenda," she replied without hesitation. Jubee gurgled in what seemed to be a sort of disbelieving gasp.

"Grenda?! The heck you want 'er, for? She's ma best!" he yelped.

"And your fastest. Please, it's important," she insisted. Jubee paused for a moment then slapped his knee.

"Fine, I'll lend 'er to ya, but only on account of y'all savin' the Rock House! And you send her right back, ya hear?"

Nora nodded slowly, but her eyes betrayed her impatience.

"Here ya go!" Jubee cried and shoved a long wooden flute, one of many like it, into her hand. "But she can only take one of ya'll!"

"That's fine," Nora replied without hesitation and raised the flute to her lips. She played four long, deliberate notes. The clear sounds of the wooden flute sailed high above the wind and the rolling waves, spreading their sound out to the surrounding area like the branches of a great and invisible tree.

Raz tapped his foot in the sand impatiently, all this talk of grave threats, the Masters, and mystical mumbo jumbo was getting on his nerves. There was a whooshing sound from behind him, quiet at first but rapidly getting closer. He dove for cover as a massive dark shape, passed silently overhead, kicking up sand and debris in its wake.

Grenda, the great owl, swooped to a stop next to Nora, towering over her. Her feathers were jet black with silver tips on the wings. The piercing green eyes were fixed into a permanent scowl. Hanging around the owl's neck was a sturdy rope. It twisted its head this way and that, surveying the destruction around it, hooting with curiosity and alarm.

"Now, now, don't you fret, girl. This here's just a minor inconvenience," Jubee comforted.

"Easy, Grenda. You remember me, don't you girl?" Nora slowly reached out her hand and scratched at the big owl's chest. Grenda nibbled at her robes affectionately.

Of the many ways the negotiation for Nora's help could have ended, escape by giant owl hadn't occurred to either Raz or Rin. So, unsure of what else they could do, they stood and gawked at Nora in utter confusion as she confidently climbed onto the big bird's back.

"Sorry to leave you two like this, but there's really no time to waste," she explained.

"Oh yeah, no time to waste," Raz repeated back sarcastically. "It's not like Rin and I are on a deadline or anything."

Nora turned to Raz and Rin, her hard frown returning. "Just remember what I said! Law low for a few days and don't do anything stupid! I'm sure it'll be fine!"

The owl spread her wings and shot into the air. She streaked across the sky back towards Crescent Isle. Raz clamored to his feet and watched them fly off.

"Fine, go ahead and leave! See if we care!" he yelled out after her as she quickly disapeared into the horizon.

The two Moonken cast long shadows that crawled up the walls of Jubee's Rock House as the sun slowly made its way lower on the horizon. It was only a few hours from sundown now. Once it got dark, Raz and Rin would officially be outcasts from Crescent Isle and enemy number one on the Red Cobra's list.

Rin lugged himself slowly to the water, plopping down in the sand with a heavy thud. Hunched over in his gray robes, he resembled a great boulder amidst the sand and scattered debris on the beach. He leaned over and picked up stones, idly skipping them across the water without purpose.

This was not what victory was supposed to look like and no matter what Nora said, Raz knew that day was undoubtedly a victory. Then again, Raz suspected that someone like Nora could be given a free house and still complain about a squeaky floorboard. It was in her nature.

With a spring in his step, he walked up behind Rin and

snatched the smooth, flat rock out of his hand mid-throw. Raz hefted it a few times and then flicked his wrist, sending the rock twirling into the bay. Lacking Rin's dexterity, the rock plunged into the waves without skipping once.

"Huh. You made that look a lot easier," Raz noted with a grin. Rin didn't return his smile. "I've been thinking. What's so great about Nora, anyway?"

Rin took his eyes off the sea and looked at Raz curiously. "What d'ya mean? You saw how she handled Nox. She was gonna help us come up with a plan," he mumbled.

"Man, if we waited for Nora to come up with a plan, we'd be as shriveled up as Master Dou by the time she finished!" Raz exclaimed and Rin chuckled, unable to deny it.

"Listen," Raz continued, "Nora thinks if we just meditate, this'll all blow over. But she's wrong. Nox is coming for us. And I, for one, am not ready to roll over and give up."

Rin picked up a stick and pushed the sand around in circles. "I don't know…" he said, his words stained with uncertainty. "We came here for a reason, right? We needed her. How are we supposed to take him down on our own?"

"What are you saying?!" Raz said and leaped to his feet. "You're my lucky charm, man! Ever since we teamed up, we've accomplished more feats of unrivaled badassery in two days than most Moonken do in their lifetime! Think about it! We took the old path to the dojo by ourselves, we went toe to toe with a Darksprite, and today we beat down an Irokomancer and an army of Iroko Minions single-handedly!"

Rin sat and pondered this for a moment, turning over in his head the whirlwind that was the last two days. He nodded slowly, and a twinkle came to his eye.

"Compared to an Irokomancer," Raz said, "Nox will be a piece of cake. Plus, we've got our secret weapon! What more could we possibly need?"

"Our secret weapon is a half pulverized big carrot?" Rin wondered and poked his finger into one of the holes left by the Irokomancer's thorns.

"No! Well, yeah, but it's not just a carrot. I think this thing worked! I feel like it... woke something up inside of me! That's why Klu gave it to me! The carrot IS the secret of Kung Fulio!"

Rin jumped to his feet, excitedly pacing back and forth, much to Raz's relief. Finally, it was feeling the way victory was meant to feel. They didn't need Nora anymore than Raz needed the use of all his limbs to fight an Irokomancer. The various avenues to Kung Fulio mastery laid tantalizing open to him now, with only Nox in the way as a minor inevitable obstacle.

"You're right! I..." Rin paused as if uncertain that the next few words were really coming out of his own mouth, "I mean, I know it seems crazy, but after seeing what you did today... I think we can take him!"

"Nora said it herself. The only reason those jackasses follow Nox is because they think he's indestructible," Raz reasoned. "And the only reason we couldn't beat him before is because we believed it! That jerk got in our heads! But with my magic carrot, Nox doesn't stand a chance!"

Rin held up his own hands in front of him and nodded as if he approved of the power he saw there. "You're right. We're not just team RiRaz, we're team RiRaz REBORN!" he exclaimed.

"Exactly," Raz agreed. "Nox expects us to run, but that's what the OLD Raz and Rin would do."

"So, what are you thinking?" Rin wondered.

"Simple, we're gonna do the opposite," Raz said. "We're gonna take the fight to him!"

He dramatically swung the carrot in front of him, kicking up a cloud of sand directly into his own face, causing him to cough and sputter.

"Maaaaaaan, I wish Klu had given me a secret vegetable, er... some kind of weapon," Rin mused.

"Don't sweat it, man, you're the ninja brains to my Kung Fulio brawn," Raz said, flexing his rather meager bicep.

"Still, I wish I could restock on my ninja ammo before we got back to Crescent Isle," Rin muttered.

"Speaking of which," Raz looked around the empty beach of Jubee's Rock House, "you don't think Jubee has another one of those badass birds to take us both back, do you?"

Rin froze as if Raz's innocent comment had set off a hundred calculations in his mind.

"That's it! Jubee!" Rin gasped as his eyes lit up with renewed vigor.

"What about him?" Raz asked suspiciously.

Rin grinned a fiendish smile. Raz had known Rin long enough to know what look meant: a scheme was being hatched.

"I got an idea! One Nox is never going to forget," Rin said then cackled mischievously.

"What are you plotting?" Raz asked.

"Heh, heh, heh. You'll see... You'll see..." Rin murmured. His face grew dark. Devious. Slowly, he withdrew Jubee's coupon out of his pouch.

"Time to go shopping!" Rin cried then took off in a sprint towards Jubee, waving the coupon above his head excitedly.

Preparations for Raz and Rin's final battle were officially underway.

CHAPTER 14
A DARK PATH

The chicken-like creature clucked nervously as it scanned the dark wooded path for movement. It heard noises from all around - horrible noises. In every shadow and behind every bush, predators lurked - sneaky, horrible predators that could snatch it up at any second and rip it apart with their—

It clucked again sharply, driving the bad thoughts away. It looked up as it bounced around in the grip of the strange, mostly hairless creature. Did it want to eat him? With its tuft of white hair on its head, this ugly bald ape was petting its head softly and speaking in soothing tones. Predators wouldn't do that.

Or WOULD they?

Deep down, there was a squawky, fiery voice calling it

to give in to the fear - to fight for its life. The very thought of such a confrontation was terrifying, which caused the chicken to shift. When it did, it grew a little larger. The color of its muddy brown feathers shimmered and took on a slight reddish tint. The voice inside of it squawked with fiendish pleasure.

Any further, and it would lose control completely.

But the big ape creature pet its head again. This felt very nice. So nice that the chicken settled down. The voice of anger and vengeance that rattled in its head fell silent. The chicken decided that the big ape wasn't a predator after all. But one must always stay vigilant.

Raz eyed the scrawny bird tucked away in Rin's arms suspiciously. The big guy had painstakingly gone over everything in Jubee's shop, even going so far as to dig up a few things from the sand. The chicken was his first choice.

It had cost him all the money he had on him, even after the coupon and Nora's employee discount. Still he considered it a real bargain.

"You sure Jubee didn't swindle you?" Raz delicately inquired.

"Nope! I'm sure! This here is a one hundred percent genuine Fury Chicken! They're pretty common around here, even you must know that!" Rin said defensively.

"If they're so common, why don't you just and catch one in the wild?"

The gentle pad of Rin's footsteps drifted away as he came to a stop, his face changed to a deathly pallor. He stared up through the trees with the vacant expression of one who had experienced far too many unimaginable, chicken-related horrors.

"They usually travel in packs..." he said quietly as if this were an adequate explanation.

It was not.

"Chickens. That travel in packs," Raz repeated, waiting for some kind of punchline that never came.

"Once, I heard an old farmer caught some chickens who'd gotten into his grain..." Rin mumbled, his voice barely audible above the sound of crickets. "Fury Chickens..."

"And?" Raz nudged Rin along. He turned to Raz, petting the Fury Chicken's head softly.

"And the farmer was never heard from again." A gentle breeze rustled the leaves of the forest trees.

As was usually the case with Rin in times of extreme stress and danger, the color quickly returned to his face, the spring returned to his step, and he cheerily strode forward. Rin was emotionally agile, he had to give him that.

Raz doubted the validity of Rin's story, but decided to focus on more important things.

The final fight with Nox was close at hand.

Even from Jubee's Rockhouse they could see the distinct crescent moon shaped mountain of Crescent Isle. At this distance, the island appeared incredibly peaceful, every bit the idyllic place it was said to be.

It reminded him of the day he'd first arrived, so full of hope, but also naive. This time he was ready. Battle-hardened. Smiling, he confidently strode along the dirt road with Rin trailing closely behind. The eastern bridge, usually the most-well traveled of all the entrances into the city, stood empty aside from two significant figures at the opposite end. Raz paused as his foot hit the first wooden plank.

On the opposite end of the bridge, barricading the gate like a brick wall, stood Bolo. Diego perched on the railing next to him like a thin, spiky-haired gargoyle.

Clunk... Clunk... Clunk...

Bolo idly flicked back and forth at the log that remained tied into his hair, creating a hollow, almost meditative sound. In stark contrast to the tattered, mud-stained robes on Raz and Rin, their custom red and black robes were spotless as if they'd changed into them just for this occasion.

Didn't waste any time, did they? Raz thought, a sardonic

smile creeping to his lips.

Bolo snapped his fingers, capturing his companion's
attention. Diego's red mohawk wobbled in the wind as
he hopped down and landed at Bolo's side. He folded his
arms in front of him in a feeble attempt to appear equally as
intimidating as the overgrown stack of muscle next to him.

A gentle wind sent leaves from the forest skittering
across the wooden planks, and made the supports on either
side of the bridge groan softly as the two groups of Moonken
eyed each other.

Rin squeaked and quickly shoved the Fury Chicken
out of sight into the safety of his robe. It didn't feel like an
ambush, but Raz readied the hand with his carrot, dropping it
down to his side, just in case. He scanned the area around the
bridge for trouble.

Bolo and Diego cocked their heads with curiosity and
strode toward them. It wasn't every day someone walked
toward the Red Cobras when they had the option to run. Raz,
too, walked
forward until the two sides stopped within ten feet of each

other.

The wind blew, filling in the silence. Tension filled the air as neither party moved to attack. Without their fearless leader, Raz noticed a hesitation in his flunkies he'd never seen before.

"Didn't we kick your asses out of town already?" Bolo grunted, extending his open palm to them.

"Yeah, where do you think you're going, fresh meat?" Diego snarled.

"Actually, we were just comin' back to see Nox, weren't we Rin?" Raz said, turning to his portly companion, who didn't answer. The chicken clucked nervously in his robe.

"Well, tough! You don't have a—" Diego paused as Raz's words finally processed in his brain. Now, he was more confused than ever. "Wait, did you say you wanted to see Nox? But he…you… huh?"

"Yeah, that's right, why don't you scamper off and get your evil master for us? Would you kindly?" Raz said casually, confidently.

Suspicious, Bolo craned his entire body to study Raz as he lacked the dexterity in his muscly neck to move his head alone.

"Seems fishy," Bolo said succinctly.

Raz's eyes turned skyward in thought. He swung the carrot idly and impatiently at his side as he tried to think of an excuse.   "Yup, well, I can see why you'd think that. But we uh… we came to… er… came to…"

"… Beg for forgiveness?" Rin chimed in helpfully. Raz swung the carrot over his shoulder again and snapped with his other hand.

"That's the one! We came to beg for forgiveness! On account of us being the… worst and whatever!"

Wind blew across the bridge once more as Diego and Bolo stared blankly at them and then at each other.

"The boss does like to see losers beg. O-okaaaaaay…I

guess…" Diego gulped, "I guess we take 'em to Nox… right?" he turned to Bolo.

"Mmm," Bolo grunted then shrugged. The Red Cobras turned away from the bridge and waved Raz and Rin onward. Diego turned back suddenly and pointed at them accusingly. "And no funny business!"

Who? Us? Raz thought wickedly and held out a fist for Rin to bump. Several embarrassing seconds of no return bump went by before Raz lowered his hand back to his side and examined his friend. Rin walked stiffly, darting his eyes across the rooftops of Crescent Isle and hugging his concealed chicken like a safety blanket. Feeling suddenly more confined, the chicken let out a sharp "BWAK!" that echoed against the walls of the surrounding buildings.

Unable to swivel his thick neck independently of the rest of his bulk, Bolo turned his entire body back to investigate the suspicious sound. Raz quickly raised his fist to his mouth and began coughing wildly, adding in a few clucks here and there to make it sound like convincing chicken sounds.

"I, uh," he coughed a few more times for effect, "got something caught my throat."

"Weirdos," Bolo grumbled, adjusted the wooden log in his hair and turned back to face forward. With Bolo's concentration elsewhere, Raz faded back a few steps and elbowed Rin in the ribs.

"Dude, relax!" he whispered, taking notice of the various citizens of Crescent Isle who stared back at them.

"We're being escorted to the Red Cobras secret hideout! How the heck am I supposed to relax?!" came Rin's raspy response.

"I don't know, walk casual!"

Rin nodded with understanding then promptly hyperventilated and started to walk with the same relaxed fluidity of a wooden coat rack. The bulge of the chicken

squirmed uncomfortably under his robes as if it had grown. Beads of sweat formed on his brow, the attempt at normal movement taking up the entirety of his concentration. A few of the late-night patrons of the shops nudged each other and pointed.

"More casual, more casual!" Raz ordered out of the side of his mouth, forcing an unnatural toothy smile.

Raz leaned closer to his nervous companion, making sure the Red Cobras were out of earshot. "Just remember, all you gotta do is distract them. I'll take care of the rest," he said and patted his carrot. "And make sure your new friend doesn't blow our cover!"

Rin nodded, and dug a free hand into his bag. "Alright,

alright. Jubee gave me this, just in case," he said and drew
out a small green berry between his thumb and pointer finger
then shoved it into his robe. The chicken pecked at the berry
suspiciously then gobbled it down. Soon, its eyes rolled back
in its head and it was fast asleep.

Diego and Bolo suddenly turned and left the market,
dipping into the back alleys. Raz and Rin followed behind
breathlessly, feeling their confidence waver as they grew
more confined. After a series of twists and turns, a pit formed
in Raz's stomach as he realized they'd ended up back at the
beginning – back to the alley where Nox had beaten him
down two days prior, where this whole mess had started.

"What're you waitin' for?" Diego said, waving them
forward. Raz stepped into the alley reluctantly. He quickly
scanned the walls, looking for exits he might have missed the
first time. If the Cobras plan was to rush them, he would be
ready this time. The two Red Cobras moved to the far wall.

"Raz… I've got a bad feeling about this," Rin
whispered, his hand already half-buried in his satchel. Raz
took a deep breath and tightened his grip on the carrot.

There was a loud scrape as Bolo moved aside a huge
chunk of rock and metal. Raz let the carrot fall to his side.

"You've gotta be kidding me," he mused aloud as he
moved to join the two other boys.

Now uncovered at the end of the alley was a squat
stone archway, half Raz's height, built right into the
foundations of Crescent Isle itself. It looked ancient, and old
Moonken symbols were carved into the outer edges. Raz had
heard rumors of the old underground tunnels, but in all his
time at the monastery, this was the first time he'd seen them.

"Get in," Bolo ordered. Raz squinted into the dark
opening but couldn't make out what was inside.

"Why don't you go first?" Raz squeaked uneasily.

But Bolo only grunted. He grabbed him by the robes
like a sack of potatoes and tossed him into the dark tunnel.

Rin's hands darted up with open palms as he willingly squeezed in behind him. Abruptly, the light from outside disappeared as Bolo slid the cover back into place.

For a moment, Raz considered the possibility he'd miscalculated and gripped the stalks of the carrot tightly.

CLICK!

A string of cheap red lights flickered to life, illuminating the walls. Raz found himself in a narrow passage, much taller than the door suggested, as if the entrance had been half-buried long ago. He stood up and saw Diego poking his head out from around a corridor up ahead.

"Don't tell me you guys are scared of the dark?" he taunted as Raz wiped the sweat from his brow.

Bolo shoved past the two dazed Moonken and gestured for them to follow. The stone walls were slick and stank of damp seawater. Apart from the lights, it had an air of antiquity, its tunnels carefully carved for those of the ancient monastic order. It reminded Raz of the construction under the old dojo, but much more accommodating, like it was once not meant to be a secret at all. The stones under his feet were smooth and worn from frequent use over the centuries. Diego confidently weaved around the maze-like passages. It was clear that he'd been here many times before.

The tunnels were expansive, stretching into paths that led all over the island. It occurred to Raz that without Diego's stiff red hair as a beacon to guide him, he might have easily become lost in the tunnels, never to be found again.

Rounding the corner, the passages gave way to a wide-open space, the dead silence of the tunnels washed out in an overwhelming cacophony of noise, light, and activity. Raz staggered into the room, struggling to get his bearings. Loud, angry electric guitar music blared from speakers, and all around him were sounds coming from dozens of various machines he couldn't identify. They lit up in multiple colors and chimed strange tunes. The stale air of that same blue smoke from Klu's Dojo flooded the room. It mixed with the musty, greasy smell unique to day-old fried food.

"Daaaaaaaaamn…" Rin marveled in dumbfounded wonder. Raz blinked dumbly against the bright lights, letting his vision slowly come into focus.

Once it did, his jaw hit the floor.

"Double Damn," Raz agreed.

"Welcome to the Snake Pit," Diego hissed with excessive bravado, baring his pointed teeth in a toothy grin.

Every square inch of the ancient space had been converted into a dreamland of mechanized and magical delights. The pleasures that were denied by the monastic order were all on display. Girlie posters lined the stone walls, wooden skate ramps painted with red and black flames, were wedged up against the ancient stone walls and overhead. Areas once painstakingly carved to serve as an area of meditation now converted into the perfect angle for a sick skateboard gap. Dozens of mechanized gaming machines were all lined up under a giant neon snake, its red tongue flicking on and off. Rarely seen outside of the biggest cities, the various game boxes flashed lights and played tantalizing tunes from little speakers to lure in potential players. The large open area had an upper balcony overlooking it, and ziplines had been set up to descend into it quickly.

Several scrolls with moving images, much like they'd seen in Klu's stash, were hung on the wall. Each featured a Moonken warrior, impossibly muscular and handsome and with the unmistakable pompadour of Nox, flexing and striking martial arts poses. Under them, tables full of cigarettes, pipes, roasted meats, fried taters, Chow Rice, dumplings, meat buns, candy, drinks, and a dozen other items had Raz's mouth watering just looking at them.

On a small table, was a black scroll inlaid with silver snakes. Rin began to babble incoherently and move towards it like a moth to a flame. He glanced over at Raz, his mouth hanging open, and pointed at it in stupefied wonder.

"A... a... a ninja banishment scroll. The real deal ... it's... it's...beautiful..." he finally croaked in between bouts of swallowing the drool that had begun to pool in his mouth. Raz noticed several other scrolls like it; some appeared to his untrained eye like more ninja artifacts, others like the Kung Fulio scrolls in Klu's stash.

Flickering light drew his eye, and he gawked in disbelief at a large metal cube that played pictures of figures locked in combat. He'd heard of these before, a picture cube, a piece of old tech dug up from beneath the Earth Shells. It was sporadic, worth a fortune, and bafflingly sitting below one of the most stoically anti-modern places in all of Speria.

Never before had he seen so much cool and rare stuff crammed into one space before. Rin looked on with what must have been jealousy, his own secret hideout put to utter shame.

However, the surprise of the lights and secret stash paled in comparison to the other main feature of the room: it was crowded. There were people everywhere, at least a dozen or more by Raz's count.

All of them wore the robes of the Red Cobras.

CHAPTER 15
A CHICKEN, A CARROT, A SHOWDOWN

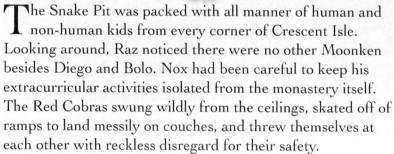

The Snake Pit was packed with all manner of human and non-human kids from every corner of Crescent Isle. Looking around, Raz noticed there were no other Moonken besides Diego and Bolo. Nox had been careful to keep his extracurricular activities isolated from the monastery itself. The Red Cobras swung wildly from the ceilings, skated off of ramps to land messily on couches, and threw themselves at each other with reckless disregard for their safety.

Raz looked to his right. A portly recruit guzzled glowing orange liquid from a jar, then spit out a string of flame, lighting the ends of six or seven cigarettes lodged in another recruit's mouth, missing his face by inches. He looked left. Three recruits sparred with each other with blunted spears while riding skateboards.

This wasn't just a hangout. It was a training ground. A

training ground for an entire new squad of Red Cobras.

Nora was right, at least in part: Nox was building an army. Right under the Master's noses. A wild energy filled the air, an excitable unpredictability that bubbled up from every person in the room. It felt dangerous. Volatile, like it might explode at any second.

How could a den so flashy and filled with so many recruits escape the Master's notice? The answer was simple, really: it didn't. It couldn't have. It was said Master Dou could hear the flapping of an insect's wings from across a room. That led to only one conclusion: the Masters knew and had chosen willful ignorance.

Among the two dozen or so people in red robes, Nox wasn't there. Raz glanced at Rin, and found his eyes still peeled to the Ninja relic on the table. Rin had become so distracted that the drugged chicken's neck had flopped out of the folds in his robes and was in full view.

"Rin," Raz snapped, keeping his voice low.

"Huh? What?" Rin replied in a daze, wiping a line of drool from his mouth.

"XYZ man!" Raz hissed out the side of his mouth, trying to point with his carrot hand subtly.

"Huh?" Rin clearly didn't understand the reference.

"X-amine Your Zipper!"

Rin patted his chest, until realizing that the limp chicken head had been flopping out of the front opening in his robes, below his rope belt. He quickly shoved it back into hiding.

"It isn't dead, is it?"

"Nooooo," he said defensively and patted his chest a few more times to make sure his hidden hen was secure. "Um, probably. Jubee might have said to only to use half a berry."

"It's still gonna… um… work though, right?"

Rin winked. It was not reassuring.

Raz's train of thought was interrupted as his hips were jarred
to the side by a Dwarf girl zipping by on the skate path. She
flew by them along with a couple of human companions.

"Oughta my way, fresh meat!" she snarled in a squeaky,
yet commanding voice.

The Dwarf eyed the new Moonken warily, her fingers
twitching in violent anticipation. Diego cleared his throat as
she kicked herself off of the board and turned her attention
to her Moonken leader. She stood at attention like a cadet in
service. The three newly arrived Cobras crossed their hands
on their chests and flayed them out in the Red Cobra Salute.

"Red Cobras fricking rule," she said with curt formality,
jamming her fist in the air. Diego simply folded his arms and
waited for her to continue instead of dignifying her with a
response.

"Umm," she searched for her words, eager to please,
"we found where that group of bandits in the South are
hiding out. We've got people staking them out, watching
their movements."

Bandits? Raz raised his eyebrows in surprise. Not what
he had imagined. What else had Nox been getting up to in
his spare time away from the monastery?

She continued, "Also, about that other thing the boss
wanted, under the the—", but Diego hissed and flicked his
eyes to Raz and Rin. It was clearly information meant for
Cobra ears only.

She darted her eyes to the floor and shuffled off. Diego
watched her go and snapped off a jerky piece he'd plucked
out of a nearby barrel. Rin subtly reached for a jerky as well,
but Raz slapped his hand. He took a deep breath, steadying
his nerves.

"Hold on." Diego grinned and cupped a hand to his ear.
"Hear that?"

All of the noise in the room seemed to get the volume

turned down. In the distance echoed the sounds of grunting, and the meaty thuds of fists against flesh. They were coming from behind the closed heavy door in the back of the room.

As they approached, the music and laughter of the other Cobras faded away. Raz's senses were overwhelmed by the sounds of fighting, the stink of sweat and blood, and a tingle of fear in the air. He heard a massive crash and a scream of pain.

"Sounds like the boss is testin' out one of the new recruits," Diego hissed.

He threw open the heavy wooden door, and the four of them
entered into a large open room. The outer edges were filled with posters of Moonken warriors, Phantom Kids drawings, and weapons - real weapons.

The center of the room was open. There, Nox stood over a bloody and battered human boy. The muscles on his bare chest bulged with each breath.

The boy was lean and wiry, barely a muscle on him, but that didn't seem to matter to Nox. He kicked him hard in the chest, sending him flying onto his back. The boy tried to stand, but Nox lifted him by the hair, bringing his face to his own.

"You think you're good enough to be one of us?!" he shouted and threw the boy backward with ease. Then he calmly walked toward him. The frightened boy scrambled back to his feet, raising his hands stiffly out in front of him. Even in Raz's limited experience, he could tell immediately that this kid was no match for Nox. Nox faked a high kick then threw a low sweep, taking the boy's legs out from under him. The boy coughed and spat out blood as his face hit the ground.

Raz tightened his grip on the leaves of the carrot and ground his teeth together. This was no sparring match, it was an uncontested beating.

"Mediocre!" Nox screamed, as if announcing his victory. "An army is only as strong as its weakest soldier." The boy

raised his bruised and
swollen face off the
floor and tried to roll
away, but Nox wasn't
having it. He grabbed
him by the leg and
tossed him across the
room again. He sailed
through the air then
tumbled roughly onto
the floor, breathing
heavily but making no
immediate attempt to
stand.

"Worms like you
make me sick," Nox
said as he spit into the
ground, mashing spots
of blood into the dirt
with the bottom of his
shoe.

Just stay down,
Raz pleaded silently
and winced at the memories of similar beatings he'd taken his
whole life.

Nox strode across the room and stood over his opponent,
who couldn't even lift himself to fight back anymore.

"Get out of my sight," Nox ordered curtly as he stepped
over the boy. He pulled a large rope attached to the wall
revealing a thin metal chute. He turned to pick up the poor
kid by the robes and threw him in, kicking it closed in a single
motion.

The sound of the boy's groans quickly grew quieter until
there was a distant sploosh. Nox chuckled to himself, and
picked up a towel to dry himself with indifference, until he

noticed Raz and Rin and slow clapped, literaly applauding their
determination.

"Well well! Look at the pair of balls on you two," he
said.   The tension released and a smile slowly crept
over his expression. "Showin' your faces on my island after -
how many times have I kicked you out now?" He started to
laugh, a thick, hearty laugh that echoed off the walls.

"Hah! At least you buttholes saved me the trouble of
hunting you down again!"

Raz took another step forward. "The feeling's mutual,"
he retorted.

Nox cocked an eyebrow, waiting with an amused grin.
Raz warily stepped into the fighting circle, carefully keeping
his distance. It was crucial to wait until the moment to strike
was right.

He looked around the room. "Pretty big place you got
here, Nox. Surprised the Masters haven't shut you down,"
Raz said and lazily passed his eyes over the room. As he
saw the door, he exchanged a quick glance with Rin, who
thankfully took the hint and quietly maneuvered himself
behind the other two Cobras.

Nox barked a humorless laugh. "Shut me down? I'm
their best student!" he boasted. Nox kicked up dust from the
dirt floor, Raz took a step back.

"Hmmm, you sure about that? Maybe someone just
hasn't had the guts to prove you wrong yet," Raz replied.
Nox extended his fingers out, cracked his knuckles, then
curled them back into fists.

"Those are big words from a Moonken who can't even
balance on a log," Nox said.

"Heh. You thought that was for real? You have no idea
what I'm capable of," Raz replied, swinging the carrot down
from his shoulder to his side. Ready for action. The air in the
room grew tense. Bolo and Diego took a step toward Raz,

but Nox held up a hand.

"Patience, boys. I got this," he chuckled.

"We'll see about that," Raz said, not taking his eyes off of Nox. "Rin!" he called out.

Rin jumped into action, just like they'd planned. He leapt into the air next to the door and then kicked the massive wooden barricade into place - locking the room from the inside. All three Cobras turned in surprise.

"Hah Hah! You numbskulls DO realize you just locked yourselves in, right?" Nox questioned as he cracked both sides of his neck in preparation.

"Or is it YOU who is locked in with US?!" Rin cried mischievously. Bolo and Diego, still confused, chuckled to themselves.

"Ohoho, you won't be laughing for long," Rin said. "Not when you see... THIS!"

Dramatically, Rin reached within his robes and tossed forth his secret weapon. The Fury Chicken streaked through the air. But its unconscious body landed with a weak thud at their feet. A deafening silence overtook the room as they stared at the limp body of the small, unconscious bird.

Raz used the distraction to shuffle closer to Nox. A few more steps and he would be in range.

Bolo poked at the chicken with his giant finger, which awakened it rather abruptly, and just in the nick of time. The chicken lunged to its feet and began darting its head frantically from side to side.

That same old voice deep inside of the chicken squawked again in rage and fury. The voice demanded it give in to the fear.

This time, the chicken obeyed.

There was an otherworldly shriek, so loud it caused Bolo and Diego to jump back in fright and clasp their hands over their ears.

Rin used the chance to slip out of range.

The bird shook. Puffs of smoke sporadically erupted from its feathers like an old malfunctioning engine. Then, it started to grow, a slight amount at first, but soon it was double the size it was before, then triple. As it grew, its feathers turned a fiery red and it let out another shriek, even more piercing than before. The claws on its legs elongated into sharp, deadly mandibles. Diego and Bolo's necks craned back as the chicken grew. Soon, it towered over every Moonken in the room. Glowing red orbs replaced the small, confused chicken's eyes. As it opened its beak to screech again, a red flame erupted.

"BKAAAAAAAAAAAAAAAAAAW!" The once tiny bird screeched as it flung out its massive, flaming wings.

"None can survive the wrath of the Fury Chicken!" Rin announced.

The wooden door rattled as Nox's army of Red Cobras barged against it helplessly to get in, but the sturdy barricade held.

Rin jumped back to safety as the Fury Chicken charged forward, clawing at the air with its massive razor-sharp talons. Diego and Bolo frantically rolled to the side. Dust billowed out from under it as it wheeled around for another charge, stamping, pecking, and breathing fire across the ground. Diego and Bolo flanked around it. They each took turns timidly inching in, but the giant flaming bird moved so erratically, they found themselves hesitating.

"Go on! What are you waiting for? It's only a chicken!" Nox ordered. "Take that thing down!"

Diego, lunged at it head-on, but the creature quickly spun around to meet him with its beak and sent him rocketing to the floor with a thunderous peck.

Bolo cracked his neck and took a hesitant step forward. As he approached, the Fury Chicken spread its wings, which erupted into flames. The large Moonken leaned back, trying to keep the highly flammable log atop his head away from

the flames. Lunging forward, the Fury Chicken constricted Bolo in its talons. Holding the large Moonken in place, the angry bird pecked mercilessly at his head. Each peck hitting the log with a loud clunk.

Meanwhile, Nox and Raz stayed on either side of the sparring hall, trying to ignore the chicken-induced chaos. From Nox's pompadour, a few strands of hair fell out of place as the master of the Red Cobras began to sweat.

Raz dug his feet into the dirt, he felt the dust swirling around him, energy drawing into the coming strike. Nox's eyes darted away from his opponent, towards the chaos at the entrance of the room. Raz smiled.

This was it. This was the moment he'd been waiting for. He lunged forward, rocketing towards Nox and drawing all his strength into the carrot as he raised it above his head.

"Hey Nox!" he called out, "Time to get some vitamin A!"

Not his best effort at an insult, but it didn't matter, the battle-hardened carrot, slayer of Irokomancers, was already swinging down towards Nox's head. Soon this whole nightmare would be over. Nox had gotten the drop on them before, but this time was different.

Nox was off-balance, distracted. It was like he had temporarily forgotten Raz existed. That was his loss. Raz watched the carrot's descent in slow motion, perfectly aligned to flatten the idiotic pompadour, and end the fight in one decisive strike. No matter how tough Nox thought he was, he would be no match for the mystical carrot. The weapon that had taken down a forest demon and its minions and smashed through a door as if it were made of tissue paper.

Then it all went wrong.

Pivoting, Nox narrowly dodged out of the way. Raz put so much force into the first blow, he found it pulling him forward and off-balance. He'd missed only by a matter of inches. The next one - that would do it. He rolled forward onto his feet then swung the carrot around, this time in a wide side arc to chop at the ribs. At that moment, their eyes met.

Nox smiled.

"HRAH!" Nox shouted and drove his fist into the oncoming carrot, striking it right at the end with pinpoint precision. The force of the punch traveled up it like a shockwave, and in a millisecond, Klu's carrot exploded in a shower of orange mushy bits, leaving only the wilted green leaves in Raz's hands. The smile still plastered on his face, Nox did not even pause before leaping across the room in a single bound, coming to a halt at the feet of the beastly bird.

"Sometimes, if you want a job done right, you gotta do it yourself," he grumbled as he leaped into the air. Weaving and bobbing his head from side to side, he effortlessly dodged a wave of frantic pecks and deflected one of the chicken's talons as it came to rake him across the chest. At the pinnacle of his jump, he sent his fist upward and struck the bottom of the chicken's beak with a vicious uppercut.

"HIGH FIVE, CLUCKSUCKER!!!" He grunted as his fist collided.

The impact sent the bird's humongous body flipping backward and crashing into the opposite wall.

Within moments, it had shrunk back to its normal size and let out a few wheezing clucks as it tried to regain its balance. Nox landed softly and dusted himself off. Casually, he threw the heavy barricade off the door, and in moments the entire army of Red Cobras streamed into the room. They surrounded Raz and Rin in a wide circle, panting heavily with anticipation. They twitched, ready to lash out like caged animals.

Shakily, Raz rose to his feet and scanned the angry faces around him. He wiped at his face where a cold sweat had broken out. Without his carrot, he had no chance. He'd completely failed - not just himself, but Rin, the other students, and every other creature on Crescent Isle that had suffered under Nox's punishing rule.

All that remained of Raz's carrot now laid at his feet. The Secrets of Kung Fulio, which had been bestowed unto him, had been reduced to a pile of sloppy orange pulp.

He stared at it in disbelief. How could it have been destroyed so easily? It was inconceivable. He crumpled to his knees and scooped up the chunks in his fingers as if he could reconstitute it and do the whole sequence of events over again. But the stringy bits simply slid through his fingers back onto the dirty floor.

All of his planning, effort, and dreams had been destroyed in just two strikes.

Nox's shadow loomed over them. He crossed his arms in front of him to flex out his shoulders.

"Well, I'll give you one thing. You two dingleberries got spunk." He grinned. "Maybe you're not entirely useless after all."

He gave a sharp whistle, and gestured for the Red Cobras to circle in.

"Tie em up boys!"

TO BE CONTINUED IN

TWILIGHT MONK: "RETURN OF THE ANCIENTS"

Available in 2021 at www.Aquatic-Moon.com

Please remember to leave a REVIEW! Strong reviews help the
author to create more books like this one.
Thanks for reading!

-Trent

TWILIGHT MONK

MORE BOOKS IN THE TWILIGHT MONK UNIVERSE

- World of Twilight Monk
(Art Book and World Guide)

- Beast of Tuksa
(Illustrated Novel)

- Escape From Giant's Crown
(Illustrated Novel)

- Secrets of Kung Fulio
(Illustrated Novel)

Printed in Great Britain
by Amazon

63868512R00132